The Masters Review
ten stories

The Masters Review

The Masters Review, Volume V
Stories Selected by Amy Hempel
Edited by Kim Winternheimer and Sadye Teiser

Front cover: Adobe Stock 68131620
Design by Kim Winternheimer

Interior design by Kim Winternheimer

First printing.

ISBN: 978-0-9853407-4-2

Printed in the USA

The Masters Review

ten stories

Volume V

Josie Sigler · Eliza Robertson · A. E. Kulze
Katie Young Foster · Jonathan Durbin
Jonathan Nehls · Andrés Carlstein · Laurie Baker
Shubha Venugopal · Kari Shemwell

Stories Selected by Amy Hempel
Edited by Kim Winternheimer and Sadye Teiser

Editor's Note

Five years is a milestone. Since its inception, *The Masters Review* has published stories by emerging writers, seeking out today's best new voices and offering a quality platform for their work. What started as a home for writers in graduate-level creative writing programs has turned into a publication that champions all emerging writers, offering their stories and essays to a growing readership. With each issue we see more submissions than the year before, a wider range of voices, and the opportunity to introduce ten new writers to our literary community.

Amy Hempel has established herself as an expert on short fiction. Her accomplishments range from a Guggenheim Fellowship to PEN/Malamud and Rea Awards for short stories. Her work has appeared in numerous collections and anthologies, *The Best American Short Stories* and *The Pushcart Prize* among them. She is the winner of the Ambassador Book Award and her work has been named a *New York Times* Best Book of The Year. The list goes on. What you'll discover in the long catalog of her biography is a career dedicated exclusively to short forms. We never expected to be so lucky as to have Amy Hempel oversee this anthology, and it feels incredibly special to mark this issue with a judge incomparable in her knowledge of short fiction.

The library of Masters Review authors continues to impress, and this year I'm proud to present ten writers of extraordinary talent. Their stories tackle war, immigration, environmentalism, race, and the endless frontier of conflict that makes up our interior lives. In Amy Hempel's introduction she writes: "I wanted narratives that overturned expectations, that gave me a much-needed respite from real life . . . " Fiction is a vessel for truth, allowing readers access to territory that the real world harnesses with limitation. It's incredible to me that visiting the world through a fictitious lens helps shape our understanding of reality. It speaks to the power and significance of stories.

I am so pleased to offer ten narratives that explore and challenge expectation. They take us to war-torn Iraq, to South Africa in the 90s, to a city in Poland on Christmas Eve. These stories also take us past the point of what we normally consider about the nature of our own jealousy, the fragility of our bodies, and the complications of parenthood. In the end, I hope you'll feel as our judge did when she read them: "rewarded."

Thank you to everyone who submitted to this anthology and to the readers and writers who helped it come into being. We are extremely grateful.

I hope you enjoy our fifth volume.

Kim Winternheimer
Founding Editor

Contents

INTRODUCTION

Introduction

The sentence is a writer's basic unit of construction. It is my way into a story, whether I am writing one or reading one. Here are some of the arresting sentences that locked down my attention in the ten stories that make up this anthology:

- They Speedo-wedgied, head-locked, and skull-knuckled each other until Jim marched out of his office wearing Hawaiians and sport sandals over bright white tube socks.

- Nor did I miss their equine, translucent daughters who asked questions such as, 'Daddy, does 'Lego' have a silent 't' like 'merlot?'

- He wanted Jack to get to know his target.

- It was too dark to see which granddaughter had come back for her, too hard to see if the other was waiting in the skirts of the trees, or had fled.

- To get past the barricade on my street I had to show my August bill to a soldier, a blond kid who looked seventeen and told me he couldn't believe how much I was paying Verizon.

- Everyone knew how they got there—Mexicans in a meat-packing town—whether they said it or not, and their knowing was a threat.

• They were trying to protect him from what he'd done.

• I was unhappy to think I could be frightened by such a man, but unhappier still, to think that his attention was something I was slow to reject.

• It felt strange listening to her advice; he'd grown accustomed to being her teacher, even after they became lovers.

• When he has walked so far that his chin skirts the surface, he says, "There are cities under here, believe it," then disappears beneath the waves.

These are stories in which normal moments are tinged with malice, characters are hiding or chasing—sometimes both, characters are looking for what might, in a stretch, be called love. Some of these stories are wild rides, and up to the challenge—as the writer Lee Clay Johnson puts it, they "don't use front-wheel drive when what is needed for this rough terrain is a 4 x 4." Others spotlight the difficulty and beauty of a number of kinds of recovery. We see the limits of wit, and why "clever" is never enough.

Back in the 1960s, Philip Roth remarked on the difficulty of competing, in fiction, with what was going on in the real world. It is no easier today—I write this after watching hours of CNN coverage of the shooting of police officers by a sniper in Dallas, after the police shootings of still more African-American men, after the Orlando massacre, and Brexit, and the ongoing presidential campaigns (I could not decide on an adequate adjective for this last).

Collected here are ten stories that rewarded my switching from current events to a stranger's imagination. I wanted someone else's thoughts in my head, but not just anyone's narrative. I wanted narratives that overturned expectations, that gave me a much-needed respite from real life with sentences I would quote to friends, and—in the best cases—stories that gave me ideas for better addressing the facts of real life that are not letting up any time soon.

—*Amy Hempel*

The Masters Review

ten stories

We Were The Drowners

Josie Sigler

It was every Dolphin's loftiest goal: to be chosen by Jim Yablonski, director of the Downriver Municipal Outdoor Pool, as one of his Drowners. From June to August, Monday through Saturday, we, the ten swimmingest members of the girls' recreational team, climbed onto our banana-seated bicycles in the first morning heat. We pedaled, streamers flowing, toward the pool at the edge of our neighborhood. We entered the beige brick building that smelled of chlorine and mildew. Tucked behind our locker doors, we undressed. In the showers, we shouted the best songs on the radio, our voices echoing, our suits sucking quick and wet against our new bodies, the dents and swells we hadn't shown to anyone yet. We reported for duty poolside at seven.

There, waiting for us in the bright Michigan sun, stood the lithest of the Shark boys, ages fifteen to seventeen, who longed to be lifeguards. They Speedo-wedgied, head-locked, and skull-knuckled each other until Jim marched out of his office wearing Hawaiians and sport sandals over bright white tube socks. A staccato screech emanated from the whistle clamped between his teeth. The boys snapped to attention, thrusting out their chests, sinewing their stomachs. Jim examined his beloved clipboard.

That morning, Rory Brunhaefer and Casey Wheldon were chosen to go first. They pulled their whistles over their heads and *rock-paper-scissored* for who got to sit in the lifeguard chair and who would walk the periphery. Casey's paper beat Rory's rock—the only way Casey would ever beat Rory as far as nine of ten Dolphins were concerned.

Casey, smirking, climbed his throne.

Jim blew an earsplitting blast.

And the drowning began.

I was a Drowner all three of my Dolphin summers. By the time I was almost fourteen, I understood the nuances of the job. There was an art to playing dead, performing the perfect accident. You had to make up a story about not only how but why you would drown and believe it in your guts before you went anywhere near the water. Each boy got just ten minutes to prove his mettle. Thus timing was of the essence if you wanted a particular boy to notice you. But so was subtlety—if you wanted him to like what he noticed.

Thus we veterans strolled around on deck, chatting and tossing a beach ball as real bathers might.

Lucy Pfeiffer, however, a newbie if ever there was one, threw her scrawny body in the water and began gulping and thrashing.

Lucy Pfeiffer. Barely twelve and considered pathetic by all. Her dad was the boss at Shyandotte Chemical. Ours was a Shy-Chem neighborhood, so most of us spent dinner listening to our dads complain about her dad. Plus everyone knew that Jim hadn't originally chosen Lucy to drown. At the awards ceremony the September before, after Jim had given out medals for speed, the coveted Most Valuable and the dreaded Most Improved, he read his list of Drowners. Lucy, unnamed, had burst into tears. Jim felt terrible, so when Charity Tremblay got sick between summers, he called on Lucy to substitute.

Charity Tremblay. Until that year, had been the most popular Dolphin. She was small and curvy. She had extra-deep dimples and her hair had once rivaled Farrah's. But you could never hate her for being perfect because she was so darned nice, looked you in the eye and listened when you talked and remembered what you said. We had been friends since kindergarten. In October, Charity started getting enormous bruises on her legs. The gym teacher, worried about what might be happening to Charity at home, spoke to the school counselor the same day the Tremblays called to say gym class was too strenuous.

Leukemia was the doctor's ruling.

We had known other people with cancer. My aunt. Kerri's grandfather. A few kids at the high school bore their radiation scars so bravely you could almost forget how their sad faces had looked on the coffee cans that graced the counters of businesses all over town. But Charity. Our leader. The one we secretly wished we could be. This was another strike against Lucy: she wasn't all that reverent about replacing Charity.

Help! Lucy called out. She spread her arms on the surface and began to float facedown.

Casey blew his whistle and shouted, Clear the pool!

He hopped from his perch, grabbed the Styrofoam rescue board, and glided toward Lucy. She wound her skinny arms around him as he hauled her out, strapped her down, and began to mimic resuscitation.

CPR was not the most important part of our sessions, Jim told us. The boys selected to become lifeguards would take an official CPR course, would perfect their pumping and breathing techniques on dummies. But learning to swim with another person in your arms? That could never be simulated. A junior high girl was the exact right weight for a high school boy to practice this on. We acted out the CPR part to give the boys a sense of the timing. The trainee would say Air! to indicate a breath instead of breathing into your mouth. When you felt sufficiently rescued, you said, Okay! That was supposed to be the end of it. But after practice in the showers, there was always conjecture about the meaning and tone of a rescue. Especially if a trainee's lips—perhaps purposely— bumped a Drowner's lips.

Lucy made Casey lean over her for five excruciating minutes. She even faked a small seizure.

Rory smiled. He'd clearly won out despite choosing rock. He twirled his whistle on its cord around his finger one way, and then the other.

Rory Brunhaefer. Almost seventeen. The Shark who held the record for butterfly. President of the high school drama club though he was only a junior. The hottest of fiddlers on the roof and ironically a Jet all the way. When the stage lights poured down on Rory—his dark curls, his hazel eyes—the whole world held its breath. Everyone said he would make it all the way to Hollywood. He had taken Charity to the movies several times before she got sick. She reported back to us that he knew everything about the business. Once Charity was off Rory's roster and a tasteful amount of time had passed, many a Dolphin began to dream of becoming the woman who would someday ride Rory's arm in *People* magazine.

Lucy was clutching her throat, moaning.

For crying out loud, Linda Peters said. It's over!

Linda Peters. The coolest Dolphin and our new leader. Unlike Lucy, Linda was aware of her change in status. She hadn't been in the pool all summer, not even for laps, and sometimes left before regular swim practice. She had outgrown the whole thing, she said. She had taken to wearing a pantsuit and sunglasses, like she was on Dynasty or something. When boys kissed her, she said like it happened all the time, it was the real deal, not part of some infantile game. Jim thought Linda was on drugs, because thanks to the war on them, adults thought drugs were the only problem a person could have. Jim had given Linda a warning: shape up or ship out. It remained to be seen which she would do. During a rescue, if you held out too long, Linda would question any claim that a boy had meant to kiss you or touch your chest. You'd be socially ruined for weeks.

Seriously, Kerri Tefferini said, tossing her hair.

Keri Tefferini. Everyone called her Tefferini. Tefferini, now second in the chain-of-cool, had an amazing last name and a football star brother also called Tefferini. She was the most paranoid person I knew.

For real, I prepared to quip, but all talk stopped as Rory walked past us on his way to the lifeguard chair.

We readied ourselves for a nice, understated drowning.

Especially me. Consensus had it that I was winning in the race for Rory's heart. He sat next to me after practice in the Dairy Queen parking lot in the twenty minutes before the high school girls arrived. He dropped by at sunset and sat with me on the porch or helped my dad water the lawn. Unlike the other drama kids, Rory didn't say much offstage, so I didn't know for sure what was happening, but Linda said it made perfect sense: Rory and I were both artists. I was going to be a famous writer. Sure, Charity was gorgeous and nice, but that wasn't enough. Rory needed someone edgy and deep.

Result? I had not been to see Charity since she got out of isolation, even when her mom called my mom and invited me. How could I explain that while she was dying I was stealing her boyfriend?

Rory climbed into the lifeguard chair and put his sunglasses on.

It was almost July. I had not yet fully drowned on Rory's watch and Lucy's embarrassing effort provided an opening to shine. So when Jim blew his whistle, I sauntered into the shallow end, letting the cool water surround me. I was careful to avoid dampening the flips I had spent an hour training into my hair. They would melt as soon as I went under, but until then I had a chance of temporarily erasing what I looked like during regular swim practice—the cap and goggles accentuated my braces and my nose, which I planned to have fixed first thing after Rory and I moved to Hollywood.

Rory's eyes swept the pool for signs of danger, resting briefly upon me. This was my chance. Before another girl could start the process, I began to sidestroke casually but territorially toward the deep end. With minimal ado, I inhaled, slipped beneath the surface, and sank to touch the pool's rough white bottom. I began to count so I could deliver an accurate report to Jim.

Rory's whistle screamed.

I felt him plunge in. His blurred but beautiful form moved toward me from above. Once he was close, in the crystalline water with sunlight pouring through, it was as if God was holding a magnifying glass to Rory. I could see the golden hairs on his arms, the sharp brown points of his nipples. I closed my eyes. His chest was hot against my back as he gathered and pulled me, stroke by stroke, to the edge. He hefted me onto the stinging concrete and rolled me onto the rescue board. His hand grazed my hip as he strapped me down. I stared at the sky. He leaned to listen for my breath, which I held—even the folds inside his ear were perfect. Water trickled from his curls onto my cheeks. He placed his hand under my neck and bent toward me.

Air! Rory barked, nearly deafening me.

He pulled away. He placed his interlocked hands a few inches above my sternum and pumped without touching me. My heart jump-started, anyway.

Air! he said again. I waited five seconds, ten, fifteen. I felt his breath on my chin. I looked into his desert-colored eyes. He smiled. Then, miracle: the curve of his upper lip touched the center of my lower lip, sending a jolt of electricity down my legs. I almost kicked him.

The angle must have been such that everyone saw. I heard a collective gasp.

Rory raised his head.

Okay! I said. I smiled and sat up, trying to appear unmussed.

Rory held out his hand and I took it. I pulled myself up. I was dizzy with conquest. He squeezed my fingers. I rubbed the chlorine from my eyes and looked at him. But he was not looking at me. No one was. All were gazing gape-mouthed at the building. What else could possibly be so almighty mesmerizing?

I turned.

There in the shade outside the glass doors stood a small girl wearing a red swim cap. She seemed to hesitate, and then walked toward us. I waited for Jim to explain to the newcomer that the pool wasn't open yet. But the girl was Charity Tremblay, our missing Drowner, minus her old curves and locks.

The drops of water running down my legs seemed to freeze. I saw a shiver pass through Charity, too. Her mother exited the building in her culottes and sunhat and Rory's fingers released mine.

A hundred eighty-seven, I blurted. A hundred eighty-seven seconds from start to finish.

But no one seemed to hear. Everyone but Linda and me gathered around Charity and said, Welcome back, good to see you, you look great.

Then Rory draped his arm over Charity's shoulders.

Mrs. Tremblay's eyes shone with proud tears, just as they had when, after Charity's second round of chemo had failed, we showed up en masse at the marrow drive with our parents in tow. We bared our veins for the needle. We knew Charity needed a miracle. We wanted to be the miracle almost as much as we wanted to run from that white room.

You made it! Jim said, chucking Charity's arm.

Charity smiled. Her dimples looked even deeper without eyebrows to distract attention from them. I could see her veins beneath skin that looked like paper against Rory's tanned arm. Charity was as skinny as Lucy, who also looked like she might join Mrs. Tremblay in crying.

Jim took Lucy's chin, tipped her face up, and said, Don't worry. I got room for all the healthy girls!

Then, Jim shoved his whistle between his teeth and we swung into action while Charity sat in a white plastic pool chair Rory set up for her. Everyone had forgotten—if they had even seen—what had happened between me and Rory five minutes before.

I looked at Linda, who shrugged. What could we do? Charity was our friend. She hadn't died. It was great news.

Soon the non-drowning members of the swim team began to arrive and practice ensued. At ten, the pool opened to the public. The real lifeguards came on duty and moms hauled water wings and coolers filled with frozen Capri Suns onto the deck. While the Tadpoles, Minnows, and Guppies splashed and belly-flopped, we changed and got on our bikes.

We rode past old plants with new names—Shy-Chem used to be Consanto Corp, Bast Chem was Americhem Solutions, and so on—past the refinery, the steel mill, the few mom-and-pop custard places in town. At the Dairy Queen, we tried to wolf down enough food to satisfy our ravenous hunger before the trainees arrived in Rory's car, a Roadmaster station wagon given to him by his grandmother when she moved into a home. The car was not-at-all-cool and everyone knew it, but at least Rory had a car, could go where he wanted when he wanted.

The boys horsed around until the high school girls arrived,

the Lady Sharks whose bodies had become too heavy to rescue. Their unbraced teeth, the perfect symmetry of the green
eyeliner we weren't yet allowed to wear and which kept them
in the locker room for twenty extra minutes so we got the
boys to ourselves also made the boys forget us. Our boys were
just a game for them. They only dated guys who had been
Sharks when they were Dolphins. Yet our boys opened the
hood of Rory's car and squinted into its bowels. The Lady
Sharks tossed their flips. They turned the radio on and up.
They did not wait for the boys to choose. They flung their
arms around the boys they wanted and danced to the best
songs of the summer.

Even Linda turned into a gawky nerd in their presence.
Thus we usually headed back to the pool where we could
realign ourselves with the Guppies for the afternoon. While
the Sharks sometimes snuck back in after the pool closed,
they never came to Open Swim. Thus, we could cannonball,
dunk each other, and scream Marco Polo without destroying
our images.

The day of our ill-fated maybe-kiss, I had just sucked up
the first bit of soggy cookie from my Oreo Blizzard into my
straw when Rory's car pulled into the Dairy Queen.

And who was in the front seat?

Charity Tremblay.

Rory opened the passenger door for Charity. He helped
her out of the car. Charity had changed into a sundress, but
she was still wearing her red swim cap.

I sunk onto the bench at the table with the other Dolphins.
Rory walked over to the window to place their order, and
Charity looked lost for a moment. Then, she headed toward
us.

It's a pity date, Linda whispered to me. He obviously likes
you.

Or, Kerri said, it's because of the whole donor thing. Maybe
Lucy's right. You really can't fight fate.

With this Kerri revived the topic that had been on everyone's lips from the time of the marrow drive until Rory started
showing interest in me at the beginning of summer. When
Charity got her marrow-miracle, the person who matched

had asked to remain anonymous. For weeks I looked into the faces of my neighbors and friends, wondering which of them was the selfless hero. I never considered that it might be one of our group. In December, during a Friday night sleepover at Lucy's house which our parents made us go to, Lucy shared her theory: Rory was Charity's match. It was the perfect teenage cancer love story. Anyone could see that. And if this was true, Rory was hers forever.

Besides, Kerri went on as she licked her cone, I'm telling you, the stuff's contagious. I know a kid at Benton who says there are four cases at his school, all from the same class. I'm not going anywhere near the pool if she does.

Tefferini, I began, wanting to tell Kerri she was being ridiculous, but Charity had arrived at our table.

Hey, she said.

It was more a question than a greeting. It was clear, somehow, that I had to be the one to invite her to join us.

Have a seat, I said.

She sat. She looked at each of us in turn and then cried, You guys! Tell me all about your lives!

When I considered my life, I could think of only two things: first, how I used to be afraid of the Connelly's German Shepherd, Duke, and Charity always walked past their yard first on our way to school and never made fun of me about it. Second, the night I learned I was not the one who could save her. How I lay in my bed feeling a rush of relief because I wouldn't have to offer up the wing of my personal ilium for the drilling.

Rory saved us from having to answer by walking over to deliver Charity's Butterfinger Blizzard. He started to say something, whether to me or Charity I couldn't tell, but just then a gang of Lady Sharks arrived at our table to fawn over Charity. One even stroked her swim cap. They had never paid attention to her before. But now one Lady Shark pulled back her coppery flips to reveal the small red radiation scars at her temples. She slapped Charity five.

Charity was back to being Dolphin number one.

For a while we tried to go to Charity's house in the evenings and hang out like everything was normal. But it wasn't the same, given Linda's glowering and Kerri washing her hands every five minutes and my anxiety that Rory would drop in. We couldn't do our hair for obvious reasons. We couldn't try on clothes because Charity's clothes didn't fit her. We couldn't talk about boys because that would mean talking about Rory. We usually watched a video until Charity fell asleep on the couch, which happened long before the rest of us were ready for sleep. The others tiptoed out the door and rode home. I usually stayed longer.

Once during this time she lifted her head, and as if still in a dream, said to me with a sigh, I just wish it was like it used to be.

It was the only time in all the years I knew her that she came even close to issuing a complaint about her lot.

When her mom came to wake her and walk her to her bed, I went home to find my porch empty. Rory didn't come anymore. And he sat with Charity at Dairy Queen.

The following day at the pool Charity would apologize, saying, I'll feel like myself again soon!

It didn't seem possible. But soon wisps of hair began to appear at the edges of Charity's swim cap. Then she switched the cap out for pretty scarves. She left her white plastic chair to sit on the edge of the pool. She dipped her legs, pretending she might slip, providing an excellent distraction to the trainees.

She's getting her figure back, Linda said, not even trying to hide her jealousy from me.

We were deep into July and Linda still hadn't drowned, nor had she gotten in the water during practice. I sat off to the side with her. I had stopped drowning as part of my plan to ignore Rory until he graduated. We hadn't talked in weeks. How could he let me go so easily?

Yeah, I said, looking down at my own hips, knowing that Rory was likely comparing me to Charity.

Linda made a face at Charity's back and scratched her eyebrow with her middle finger.

Jim, who happened to look up right at that moment, marched over and pointed at Linda, then at me, and blew his whistle. Hard.

In the pool, he said, stabbing his thumb at it. Now.

Everyone was watching. Everyone probably knew why I was moping. It seemed far less embarrassing to go along with Jim than to resist. I walked toward the pool. I didn't pause at the edge. I just let myself fall in. I decided I'd make Rory think I was drowning and rescue my own self. Proud of this plan, I surfaced to see Linda was still standing against the wall with her arms crossed and her eyebrows raised.

I'm going to have to let you go, then, Jim said, clearly thinking this would change Linda's mind.

Fine, Linda said.

She stood and stalked toward the women's locker room. The glass door swung wildly behind her.

Jim pressed his lips together and shook his head. You could see him thinking it: Drugs.

I pulled myself from the pool. The pavement was hot against my feet. I walked into the locker room. Jim didn't stop me, perhaps deciding it was better to have one kid talk another out of taking drugs. Linda was sitting on the wooden bench, her face in her hands. I sat down next to her and put my arm around her.

Linda, I said. I bent to try to look her in the eye.

What? she said, keeping her face covered.

Just let it go, I said. It's not so bad to be you. I mean, look at Lucy Pfeiffer. You could be her.

It's not that, Linda said through her fingers.

What, then?

She kept crying.

Linda, I mean it. Just get into your suit and go out there and get in the pool. You'll feel better.

At that she yanked her hands away from her face and stood as if to say, Oh, yeah? She ripped off her light yellow jacket and threw it on the floor. She pulled down her pants and kicked them aside. I stood looking at her arms and legs, which were covered with dark bruises the size of grapefruits—maybe a bit smaller. But everything cancerous, I learned when my aunt was sick, is relative in size to a grapefruit. The bruises actually looked more like bullseyes, deep red in the center, black at their edges.

Oh my God, I said.

Yeah, she said, her voice echoing against the tiles.

I held Linda, let her cry in my lap like a Minnow.

Don't tell anyone, she begged.

We have to, I said. Look at Charity. She got better. And you'll get better, too.

My family's not like Charity's, Linda said.

I knew as well as anyone that Mr. Peters had a girlfriend and a wife. So I promised.

Linda and I headed to Dairy Queen together, where we shared a banana split.

You know, Linda said through a mouthful of whipped cream and cherry, I've . . . I've never even been kissed. I'm still jealous about you and Rory.

Don't be, I said. It was nothing.

Yeah, but I'm going to die without kissing anyone, she said. Then she straightened her shoulders and added, I accept it, though. It's easier to just accept things.

I guess, I said, thinking of Rory.

We spent the rest of the day riding our bikes up and down the streets of our neighborhood like we had when we were Guppies. After we parted ways, I doubled back toward the pool. I was relieved to see that Jim's Valiant was still parked out front. I let myself into the building and went to his office where I stood before him, broke my promise, and told him about Linda's bruises.

You saw them? Jim asked, clutching his whistle.

They looked just like Charity's, I said.

I sat with Jim while he called Linda's parents and told them what I had seen. She was going to be furious with me. Jim called Mrs. Tremblay, too. He thought the Tremblays might be able to give the Peters some pointers. Jim always talked as if he were coaching someone.

Jim added, Mary Peters has had a rough time of things . . .

He drifted off, not wanting to say anything bad about Linda's father in front of me.

Then he said, I know. With any chance, it will turn out to

be nothing. But if not . . . well. We can only hope the magic Charity and I had will happen for Linda, too.

I was stunned. Jim was the one who had saved Charity's life. He was her match. Which meant . . . Rory wasn't. So theirs was not the perfect teenage cancer love story. And I was potentially the worst friend on Earth for even considering this at that particular moment.

Yes, yes, Jim said. Will do.

With that he hung up the phone.

You did the right thing by telling me, he said.

Sure, I said, and went home.

Linda was diagnosed three days later.

Two weeks later, Lucy Pfeiffer's nose started bleeding during another life-saving session with Casey. Jim pressed a towel to her face, and when he drew it away, it was saturated. He told Casey to call 911. As the sirens approached, I stared at the bright tendrils of Lucy's blood that floated lazily in the sparkling turquoise water.

The day we got word about Lucy, I stayed after practice and sat in Jim's office, unable to go home and face my empty front porch.

Jesus, Jim said, running both hands through his orangey high-and-tight. If cancer was Christmas bulbs, we could decorate a tree.

I snorted. He always said things like this.

They call it a cluster, he said, when there's an epidemic.

Yeah? I said.

On sitcoms and soap operas only one character got cancer, and that character was the cancer character. Everyone else was guaranteed safety. Especially the faithful friend. The spurned lover. The messenger.

We were gathered in the locker room the next day when Kerri started the whole business about contagion again. She wouldn't get into the pool while Charity was in it, wouldn't sit on a bench if Charity had sat on it.

Think about it, Kerri whispered. She comes back, and right away Linda comes down with it, and then Lucy.

The others nodded.

Tefferini, it's scientifically proven not to be a germ, I said. It's just a coincidence.

We have to tell the boys, Kerri said. We're swimming in the same tainted water. They should be warned. And you, Kerri said, pointing at me, should warn them.

Me? Why me? I squeaked. I don't even believe it.

You're the one Rory really loves. Maybe he'll listen to you.

I had been looking for an excuse to talk to Rory, anyway, to put the whole thing behind us and reclaim some dignity. Any drama would do, I supposed. So while the others went to Dairy Queen, I waited for the boys to come out of the building.

When they did, I stopped Rory and said, Can I talk to you?

Ooo-ooo-ooo, the other boys wailed.

Rory tossed his keys to Casey and sat in the grass with me as Casey gunned Rory's engine and drove off with the rest of the boys making dirty gestures out the windows.

Rory looked into my eyes. I had forgotten how nice that was.

I thought you weren't talking to me, he said.

Well, you're too busy to talk to me, I said. Now that Charity's better.

Not really, he said. I just thought you were mad at me. You seemed mad.

It's Tefferini, I said. I began to relay Kerri's theory in a dull voice.

Thirty seconds in, Rory leaned back, slapped his hands down on his knees, and said: What a crock. Tefferini is a real piece of work.

Yeah, I said. She's going to make it really hard on Charity. I know you're . . . close. So I thought you should know.

Linda might have thought I was "edgy and deep," but this is what I thought of myself: I played it both ways. Tefferini would give me points for playing messenger, and Rory would think I was humane.

Charity's not totally out of the woods, Rory said, so she could use some decent friends. That's what I've always appreciated about you. You're not like those other girls.

It was the most he'd ever said to me about what he thought

of me. But maybe, I thought, he felt the same kinds of things about Charity.

Want to walk over together? he asked.

Sure, I said.

As I sauntered into the Dairy Queen parking lot with Rory, I wondered if Charity would be jealous. But she wasn't. She made room for both of us at her table. We laughed a lot. It was almost normal. And what if, I wondered and hoped, by sitting with the two most beautiful humans all of us knew, I bumped Tefferini out of the number two popularity slot as fast as she'd slid into it? Then maybe people wouldn't listen to her so much.

But everyone did listen to Kerri.

The girls developed new safety rules. No one could get dressed behind a locker door. If someone had bruises, it should be public information. All of the girls waited for Charity to leave before they got in the showers, which they did one at a time, in case someone was secretly infected. Obviously, no one went over to Charity's house.

The boys were worse. A few Porpoises outright quit. Todd Walters had done the math, and kids who did summer swim got sick more often than kids who didn't. Plus, he said, he heard cancer had gone gay in New York, and he certainly didn't want anything to do with gays.

I did not follow the rules, nor did I pay attention to anyone's nonsense, though my reason was not solely kindness. I wanted to please Rory, but that wasn't the whole of it either. Even if this was an epidemic-type story, I was the one who survived to tell the tale. I felt increasingly secure in my status as faithful friend, and by those terms, I could possibly *prevent* myself from getting cancer by showering with Charity. Especially because I might also be spurned.

But I wasn't. In early August, at the beginning of the horrid heat wave that would last for the rest of summer, Rory knocked at our door one evening just as it got dark.

Want to go for a swim? he asked.

I nearly fainted.

Sure, I said, trying to smile confidently.

I told my mom I was going to Charity's. She didn't stop me

despite the hour. I had told her how the others were treating Charity, and she was proud of me for doing the right thing.

I walked out to the Roadmaster and got in. Rory drove the long way, along the row of abandoned warehouses between the railroad tracks and the river. You could tell how many times a factory had changed hands by how many different kinds of windows it had. Some were blue, some green, some grey with soot, some new and clear. Smokestacks billowed their bitter clouds in the night and the air smelled like an old battery. Looping back along the river, we approached the pool just as Jim's Valiant was pulling out. Rory tucked his car along the nearest curb and killed the lights. Luckily, Jim did not see us. He'd been trying to catch the night swimmers for years.

He's working late, Rory said.

He's pretty upset, I said.

Who isn't? Rory said.

We got out of the car and Rory led me behind the building. He showed me how to scale the fence. Dropping down on the other side, we crossed into another world. Reflections from the street lamps danced on the surface of the water, but it was too dark to see into the depths. It was silent and the hot air pressed on me. Rory slipped his shoes off, tugged his shirt over his head.

He paused and said, I've actually never been here with a girl before. I mean, like this.

I answered by pulling my shirt off. I was glad I had worn my new bra.

We removed our shorts and stopped at our underwear. Rory's were no different, really, from his Speedo. Yet I trembled to see those burgundy tighties with their gray elastic band.

I dove in and Rory followed, hardly leaving a ripple. He caught up with me in the very center and we swam around each other in circles. Shaking, Rory took my naked waist in his hands. And he kissed me. A real kiss. It wasn't a trick, a performance for our friends. We kissed until we couldn't tread anymore. Then we swam to the side where I splashed Rory and he dunked me. When I came up he pulled me in and kissed me again. That time, it didn't even seem strange.

It seemed we had always been kissing somewhere in history. That night, after Rory drove me home, I lay in my bed, damp and knowing that Rory Brunhaefer was mine.

During the final weeks of that summer, when it came time to drown, Charity and I were the only ones who leapt in. I really had to hand it to her: Charity Tremblay was no spoilsport. She had taken the unspoken but clear news about me and Rory well, and we were actually having fun together in the pool again. We came up with increasingly interesting drownings, but nothing we could do was enough to make up for the absence of the others, who stood sweating on deck. It was over ninety degrees every day that August, and the day Jim finally lost it, it was pushing a hundred.

Come on, ladies, Jim said.

He was worn thin, having learned a few days before that one of his favorite Guppies had been diagnosed with lymphoma.

No one moved.

Jim threw his clipboard on the pavement and shouted, What in the Sam Hill is wrong with you girls?

We'd never seen him throw anything, especially not something so sacred as his clipboard. He picked it up, smoothed his papers, and said, Nevermind. Don't get in. It's probably best anyway.

We looked at each other. What did that mean?

That night I stayed at Charity's and on my way to the bathroom I saw an incredible thing: Jim was sitting at the Tremblays' kitchen table. I supposed that through the whole donor process he had become friends with the Tremblays. Beyond one run-in at the grocery store, I personally had never seen Jim anywhere but the pool. Further, he was wearing jeans, not Hawaiians, and he did not seem to have his whistle, though his clipboard, only slightly scarred, sat before him on the table. Mr. Tremblay was looking down at it. Mrs. Tremblay was slumped against the fridge. I stood in the dark hallway listening to their conversation.

It's been going on for years, Jim was saying, but it's getting worse.

Water? The water did it? Mrs. Tremblay asked, biting her lip.

These plants have dumped their . . . crapola . . . in the river above us. Then the sanitation plants suck it up and we go and fill the pool—

What if you're wrong? Mr. Tremblay said. This is our bread and butter you're talking about here.

What if I'm right? Jim said. It's the only common factor. These kids are in that water all day.

We have to close it, Mrs. Tremblay said.

I returned to Charity's room where she was putting on lip gloss.

Jim's here, I said.

She nodded and pressed her shiny lips together.

They're going to close the pool, I said.

What? she said, turning. They can't. It's like . . . at the center of everything.

But they did. Because it was at the center of everything.

But before they closed our pool, before they sent the water off in a test tube and the results came back, before the lawsuits and the appeals and the waiting, before we learned that a corporation with a new name isn't required to pay the price for old sins even if nothing else has changed, before Charity relapsed and Kerri was diagnosed, we got in one last drowning.

Rory was on the chair the next morning with no one to save. We were lolling around, not talking. Even Charity and I stayed on deck. That morning as we walked by Jim's office we saw him printing a sign that said: POOL CLOSED UNTIL FURTHER NOTICE. So we knew it was real, not some shared nightmare, at least not one that happens while you're sleeping.

Five minutes into Rory's turn, he shaded his eyes and looked at the building. We turned and the silence became a hush.

Linda stood behind us on the concrete, as timid as Charity had been the day she returned to us. But Linda's story wasn't like Charity's. She hadn't come because she was well again. There was no miracle-match for her. Tufts of hair clung to her scalp and bones jutted beneath her skin. She had come, she said, to drown one last time.

Next year, she said, I'll be a Shark, so this is my last chance.

I don't know, Jim said. Your mom know you're here?

Yes, she said.

We could tell she was lying. So could Jim. But he blew his whistle anyway.

As she walked past me, Linda squeezed my arm with her bony fingers, and I knew she had forgiven me for telling Jim about her, that it didn't matter anymore. Then she lowered herself into the pool. I looked at Charity. One last time, her eyes said. What did it matter now, after so many times? We plunged in.

Come on, I said to the others.

Kerri shook her head.

No way, she said.

The others stood at the edge, looking at Kerri, and then at me and Charity. Then all at once they clamored into the pool for the final swim of our childhood.

We were rough with each other, splashing and screaming and cannonballing until Linda slipped beneath the surface.

Rory blew his whistle, made his way toward her. He pulled her gently to the stairs and walked up them with her draped in his arms. The rest of us climbed out, our skins slaked and poisoned one last time. Rory lay Linda on the rescue board. He leaned over her body.

Air! Rory said.

Then he waited. He put his hands over her heart, on the breastbone that rose up like a sharp kite against the sky of her dusky skin.

Rory looked up at me.

I nodded.

The next time he bent over Linda and said Air!, my Rory touched his lips to hers.

But ours was no fairy tale. Linda lay there until Jim bent down and put his fingers against her neck.

Linda, he said.

She didn't move. She didn't take a breath.

Come on, Jim said, and then, kneeling down before her, Linda, sweetheart.

Do something! Kerri said.

Call 911, Casey said.

I started to cry. This was Linda. Linda Peters who tried so

hard to hide under a pantsuit what she knew would hurt and frighten the people she loved.

Linda opened her eyes, then, let out the breath she'd been holding.

I just had to know what it would be like, she said.

Three months earlier, she would have meant that she wanted to know what a kiss from Rory would be like. But we understood what she meant now: she wanted to know what it would be like to be dead.

Jim knelt and gathered her up. He took her in to call her mom. It was all he could do. Jim could not save Linda. He could not save Lucy, nor her little sister, nor the Guppy whom I didn't even know, nor the two Minnows who were diagnosed that fall. No one could. Nor could anyone save the great Rory Brunhaefer, my first boyfriend, who did not make it to Hollywood after all.

The Pirates of Penance

Eliza Robertson

He had taken us to the exotic meat restaurant in Fitzrovia. They lit the tables with candles in fishbowl glasses. The red paint and tapestries on the walls made us feel intimate, though Seb had failed to close on the penthouse in Battersea, and Lidia and I hated each other. Alastair sat at the head of the table—or was the table square? He had a way of sitting at the head of any table, even square ones. His tailbone inched forward, spine sickled against the chair back as he considered the inhale from his electronic cigarette, though technically we weren't supposed to vape in here. Seb had assumed the inverse position—bent over his menu, hand wedged in his hair, pit stains blotting the shirt under his cashmere cardigan. Lidia sat between them, a hand on each of their thighs, and said, Boys, chill out, shall I get the crocodile or ostrich? The phrase "chill out" sounded misplaced on her tongue. I felt oddly protective of it, not that I said "chill out," but you know, as the only American.

I had been feeling cruel since Art left—wishing small ills upon others, pleased when a raging child in Hyde Park got splattered with seagull shit. It had been six days, and I still hadn't told anyone he'd left.

Lidia pushed a few blond strands from her eyebrows. What will you get, Heather? A salad?

She spoke perfect English, but continued to pronounce my name *Hay-der*. I didn't correct her and scanned the menu. I knew already Art would have ordered the smoked python. He figured himself a sort of Indiana Jones. For example, we took our honeymoon in East Africa. It had felt problematic to purchase a luxury safari organized by the English company that planned his parents' holidays sixty years earlier, but when he surprised me with the booking, all I could say was, *You know it won't be like Hemingway. They don't let you shoot them.*

Lidia's salad comment was barbed, I knew. Dining had become political between us, a display of how much or how little we consumed. Today I would surprise her by ordering something gruesome. I'd been eating meat in Art's absence: a vengeful gesture I would mention next time he texted. *All these years you wanted to share lamb or rabbit—look at me now! Nom nom nom! Look at me now!* I had started smoking again by the same logic.

As the waiter approached our table, Seb loosened his collar and fanned the menu against his throat. He had a fuller figure than Alastair—fat, really, though he took to weights last year and now appeared as one continuous muscle. Alastair, by contrast, was an emaciated badger—tidy limbs, pointed face, even a shock of white in his otherwise loamy quiff. Not uncharming. Both of them. But money talks, etc.

You ready? asked Alastair as he reached for my menu. Our fingers grazed, his hands softer than mine.

The waiter arrived. I ordered the python. After everyone ordered, Alastair said to me, Aren't you vegetarian?

I didn't answer his question directly. I pulled a long sip of the Malbec, then filled everyone else's glasses, though I knew Lidia preferred white.

Arthur left, I said.

The table quieted. When I looked up, a crease of worry dented Lidia's forehead. I placed the bottle within arm's reach, between the peacock feathers and an astrolabe.

Thailand, I said, as though someone had asked. Where I

have reason to believe he is fucking underage sex workers.

Lidia dropped her glass, somehow catching the stem before the wine spilled. Seb choked on his own saliva, which is what I did too when I found out. Alastair leaned back in his chair, impressed, well-moisturized fingers tenting before his nose. I drained the rest of my wine and played with my butter knife on the tablecloth.

Anyway.

It is a credit and criticism of British social manner that a conversation so swiftly recovers from news like that. They asked the obligatory questions—What happened? How much reason to believe? Have you heard from him? What will you do for Christmas? But by the time the waiter delivered our starters and recharged our glasses from the second bottle, the topic had progressed to the success rates of CBT and other counseling.

This may come as a surprise to you, said Lidia, but I have taken some cognitive behavioural therapy in my lifetime, as well as hypnosis, and both worked wonders.

I drank darkly from my wine glass.

After dinner, we walked back to the office on Harley Street, where we rented the ground floor of a Portland stone Queen Anne revival. Alastair's office occupied the former study; the rest of us shared the interior reception room, each with our own oak desk slotted against the wall or side window. We met clients in the room at the front of the house, where we asked them to sit on our bespoke chesterfield or egg-inspired armchairs and poured them cups of coffee selected by myself from a cafe that roasted their own beans and cycled them from SoHo. I had accidentally left a file open on my computer—a couple from Beirut seeking a family home in Knightsbridge. Alastair assigned me the Middle Eastern clients because I spoke passable Arabic—in fact he'd hired me for this reason, though so far my clients preferred to communicate in English. I'd lived in Dubai for a few years after college, or as my mother liked to tell people, I moved to *fucking Arab Las Vegas instead of taking the LSAT*, which demonstrated I had zero skills in qualitative or quantitative analysis in the first place. After three years gluing eyelashes onto the wives of Saudi oil barons, one of my flight attendant friends introduced me to her ex, Alastair, who was starting a property firm that hunted rare homes and paired them with the über-rich. I came from different stock, let's say, but I interviewed well and spoke three languages. Art was my second client.

I was drunker than the others at the office and took time organizing my desk so no one would see me weave to the tube station. Seb squeezed my shoulder on his way out, said to ring if I needed anything. We both knew he didn't mean it. Alastair raised his hand in salute from the doorway. On the other side of the room, Lidia rifled unconvincingly through her handbag. She had pinned her hair so the waves framed her cheekbones, and in her china-green dress with the jewel neckline, she looked expensive, like a Whistles mannequin.

Hay-der, she said.

I turned back to my monitor, pressed the keys to shut the computer down. Mhm?

Will you be on your own for Christmas?

Looks that way.

What will you do?

I shrugged. Order a take-away. Watch John Cusack.

She pressed her thin, frosted lips together.

You can come home with me if you want.

I straightened too quickly and found myself groping the desk for balance. Our mutual hostility was an unspoken truth in the office, like the fact that most of our clients were scumbags.

To Poland?

If you want.

For Christmas?

I fly from Stansted on the twenty-first.

*   *   *

I didn't want more wine, but I'd acquired the ritual of opening a bottle from Art's collection every evening he was gone, like an extravagant advent calendar. An extrav-advent calendar,

I thought, as I wiped crumbled cork from the mouth of a 1985 *Château Latour*. When I'd advertised this property six years ago, I'd described it as an elegant townhouse, over seven-thousand square feet with a west-facing courtyard and adjoining mews. Inside, each room was *suffused* in natural light, as requested by Arthur, who suffered from a self-diagnosed seasonal affective disorder. I sat now in the living room that overlooked the courtyard. Out the bay window, a fox stiffened under the garden table, his eyes glinting like anchovies. We watched each other for a moment before he darted into the hedge.

Arthur didn't let me raise a finger inside—he had a "highly loyal decorator"—so the sitting rooms were done with that carpet so ubiquitous in posh houses: champagne colored, an exceptional thread count. I perched with my wine on the windowsill—I could never really sit in his furniture—and considered Lidia, why I disliked her, why women disliked each other. She found me austere, I could tell, and I found her insubstantial, but it was more than that. I feared, as I shifted my position on the sill to search for the fox in the hedge, wine lurching up my glass, spilling onto the carpet, no, I knew, that I would like her if she were ugly. I read once about a study in which women smelled the t-shirts of another woman who was ovulating and their testosterone levels rose—for aggression, the scientists thought, the hormonal equivalent of baring their teeth. Not that Lidia flirted with Art, though I remembered a staff Christmas party, one of the few he'd attended. I watched them chat at the champagne table for a minute before I joined them. Lidia excused herself for a cigarette. As she walked away, he said, *You know, I've never married a blonde.* But that was Art. He liked to rib. It annoyed me minimally at the time.

Women are not bred to bear our teeth—the opposite—we protect our wombs, the study went on to say. So while men compete in the open, in fun or with fists, women do so silently, our hostility spreading like green mold over shoes at the back of a closet. I set my glass down and drew the phone from my pocket, ignoring a text from Art on the screen, my fingers heavy with wine. I searched for Lidia in my contacts. She answered on the third ring.

. . . yeah? she said, as though I'd called from the next room. I'll come with you to Poland.

She paused. After a moment, she said, You will?

I wondered if I had made a mistake. If she had asked me out of politeness, not as an olive branch in my time of need. Instead of hesitating, or adding, *If the offer's still open. Have you asked your family?* I said, Yes. A thudding, unretractable *Yes* and thanked her for the invitation.

I'll forward you the flight details, she said.

We hung up. I wondered again where the fox had scuttled, if the Belgravia foxes hated the Mayfair foxes. Art's text said, *Do you need money for the mortgage payment? Here's Barry's number.*

I ignored the message and weaved a path from the living room to the kitchen, bowing over the butler sink to suck water from the tap, paddling cool palmfuls into my mouth. The problem is, I loved him. I didn't marry for money like everyone thought.

We celebrated our fifth anniversary in October. He had to see a client in Zurich, but would meet me in Interlaken. He booked a spa hotel; we would go skydiving. The afternoon he arrived, I opened his iPad to film the skydivers while he asked the concierge about the Matterhorn. I'd wondered about the screaming when I walked from the train station—at first I thought they were birds, a committee of vultures in the spruce trees. Then a body fell out of the sky. He landed twenty meters from me in the park. You could watch them from our balcony—the men and women dripping onto the grass in skullcaps and jumpsuits. My phone was in my purse on the other side of the room, so I lifted Art's iPad and punched in his passcode, 1111. A Safari window was open. The site sold teenage porn. A video was paused at seven minutes, where a girl dressed like Sailor Moon lay crimped on a mattress. A man crushed her chin to the foam and rammed her from behind, her hip green at the bone from thumbprints.

I did not lose my senses—I stared at the screenshot long enough to determine the girl was over thirteen, just, and to note Art's log-in: *takeachance.* I considered searching for other applications with this handle, to prove his infidelity, if applicable, but instead I closed the iPad and replaced it on the bed. I ordered a room service coffee that cost twelve Swiss Francs, then sat on the balcony to watch the bodies fall. A few minutes after my coffee arrived, the bedroom door opened and closed. Then the balcony curtain swished behind me. He greeted me with his palms on my shoulders. I imagined his hands fastening around my throat and stood with my coffee, paced back inside. He turned after me, his eyebrows lifted in hurt or confusion. He had not shaved in a day or two, and I hated then how handsome he looked. He had been wearing his hair long lately, like an Italian, the way it swept over his ear.

Do you want my biscotti? I asked.

No thanks.

My eyes fell involuntarily to his iPad. He followed my gaze. Before he could preempt me, I said, Have you seen my phone?

No.

I can't find it. I crouched and lifted the bed skirt. I guess you don't lose your devices often, I said to the dark beneath the wood frame. You're more organized than me.

I guess, he said.

I sat back on my heels, scrutinized his expression for a sign of nervousness or guilt. The thick skin above his eyes made him squint, as though blinking in sunshine.

And no one borrows them, do they? No one borrows your phone or iPad?

What's this about?

I wanted to film the skydivers, I said.

He shifted his weight, brushed a nonexistent grain of lint from his sleeve. And?

A bitter laugh escaped my throat.

Enough games, Heather.

I wanted to inform him that *I* would decide when the games were enough, but I'd grown tired too, aware of an ache moving into my eye sockets.

Someone is fucking a barely menstrual Sailor Moon on your iPad, Arthur. Possibly up the ass, I can't tell, but she doesn't look conscious.

I could see the calculations on his brow—whether he could

explain his way out of this, his mouth clamped together as if pressing an almond between his lips.

Ah, he said. Yes.

Yes?

On the one hand, he didn't think I was stupid. On the other, how could he say yes so casually? Like he had come to terms with his depravity—does this count as depravity?—long ago.

Is it even consensual?

Of course. It's all staged.

She could be your granddaughter.

I don't have kids.

I released another acidic laugh.

Hey.

Do you like Asian girls in particular?

No—

But they look younger, don't they?

They're harmless fantasies, he said. Healthy even. Oh, you're upset. Come here, baby. I love you so much.

Two months and four therapy sessions later, he flew to Bangkok.

*　　*　　*

On December 21, I met Lidia outside the M&S at Stansted Airport, where she was buying chocolate reindeer for her nephew and niece. I thought the city we were flying into might be pronounced "Lodz," and had joked this way in our correspondence, signing one email, *Łódź of love*. Now, as we pushed toward security, cabin suitcases in tow, she said, It's pronounced "woodge," by the way.

What?

Where we're going. It's pronounced "woodge."

My cheeks heated and I walked faster, dodging a pregnant woman's luggage trolley, the comeback *woodgen't you know it* slotting onto my tongue after the moment had passed. We looked an incongruous pair—Lidia in her eggshell jumper with a kangaroo pocket, where she kept dipping her hand to check her passport. Me in my wide trousers and tunic, which might have appeared clownish if not black and Scandinavian, my hair parted severely down the center.

It became clear, on the plane, that I was the only passenger who did not speak Polish. An elderly woman sat beside me, tucked in a quilted jacket she did not bother to unzip. She spoke to me in Polish as the plane taxied. I apologized, explained that I did not speak Polish, and she frowned, repeated what she'd said more urgently.

I'm sorry. English? I said.

She reached toward her air valve. I wasn't sure if she wanted the air pointed toward or away from her.

Do you want it on? I asked, stretching to touch the knob.

She blocked my hand and repeated, once more, her desire in Polish.

Sorry, I said.

Speak Polish, she said.

I don't know Polish, I said, searching the cabin for Lidia.

She batted her hand at me.

Once the plane had taken off, and I was listening to a podcast on gut flora, she spoke again. I removed an earbud. She offered me a boiled sweet from her purse.

Thank you, I said. How do you say "thank you" in Polish?

She understood and said something I interpreted as, "jin-cool-ya."

Jin-cool-ya, I said, nodding graciously, gesturing my sweet.

She shook her head and corrected my pronunciation. I tried again. Eventually, she turned toward the window and snapped photos of the clouds, each shot framed by the tip of the plane's wing.

Lidia's sister Hania met us at the airport. She and her husband lived on the fourth floor of a renovated tenement building fifteen minutes from city center. It was a nice flat—crisp wood floors, built-in bookshelves, a Swedish-looking sofa, but no larger than five hundred square feet. Hania and Dawid would sleep in the playroom with the kids and their turtle, Baron. Lidia and I would take the Swedish sofa, which pulled out, to my surprise. Or an air mattress, said Hania. Whichever we preferred.

Over the next three days, they cleaned. I don't mean they circled the house for errant shoes or magazines and ran a vacuum over the carpet so no guest embarrassed them with allergies. I mean they *cleansed*. In more ways than one, because on Christmas Eve Day, they tried not to eat too, though Hania kept offering me soup. In the living room, Lidia had opened the windows so they pointed out like fish gills. Together we polished each square of glass, leaning over the sill to reach the outside panes, continuing our conversation above the icy street. Behind us, seven-year-old Basia encouraged the turtle to scale her younger brother's back. Aron laughed and squawked syllables I could not understand, then reached his threshold of overstimulation and erupted in tears. On the windowsill between Lidia and me, my mobile lit up, as it had once or twice a day since our arrival.

Him again? she said.

I leaned farther over the sill, as if that would muffle her voice, and examined my pane with great scrutiny.

You've not responded?

I reached for the next pane, sprayed more Windex, considered what would happen if the bottle slipped from my hand and burst on a dog walker's head.

You should reply. He must be worried.

When I didn't answer, she added, You should be together for Christmas.

I shrugged. I had been thinking recently about our sex life, how we didn't *role-play*, but he wanted me to act uncertain. He would invite me onto the sofa, pour me a drink I hadn't asked for and say, *Do you mind if I smoke?* Then he would talk idly about art or politics, across from me on his armchair, until the conversation turned to a book or record he'd like to show me, enabling him to sit beside me on the love seat, the cuff of his jacket brushing my neck. All this after years of marriage, and I didn't protest at the time—thrill of the chase, I supposed, so I went along with it, asked questions when expected, played the ingenue. Now I wondered if it was practice. If he wanted to refine his techniques at rapport-building, encouraging a climate of trust between himself and Sailor Moon, guiding the conversation onto topics of sex so invisibly, the girl might think she initiated them herself, a light shame reddening her neck. He would inch nearer to her on the sofa, escalate his intensity of touch, a hand on her thigh. That was the game we played. The thought now made me sick.

What does it say at least? said Lidia.

I have to go.

I was on the sidewalk, my boots half tied, fur hood of a parka hooked over my head when I realized I was still clutching the bottle of Windex. I could not go back yet, not after such an exit, so I tied my boots and walked around the block, Windex bottle clenched beneath my coat, which I continued to wear like a cape. A man strode ahead of me with a bloodhound. The vision of the Windex bottle smashing a pedestrian's head returned to me, this man filling the lines of the faceless dog walker I had conjured. I felt guilty and smiled when he glanced back to cross the street. I crossed too, then inadvertently followed him around the corner, back to the apartment.

When I reached the front door ten minutes later, Lidia was sitting on the stairs with two cups of tea. She passed me one without speaking.

Thanks, I said. *Jin-cool-ya.*

I'm sorry you're going through this. She rested her palm on my back, though I could not feel it through the down of my parka. The tea smelled soothing—lemongrass, too hot to sip but I hovered my face over the cup, steam coating my nose.

Sorry I stole your sister's Windex, I said, setting the bottle below us on the step.

She laughed—a sharp bark, which endeared me to her, like when a beautiful person farts in public.

You've been generous.

She batted her hand at me as the old woman had on the plane.

Arthur is attractive for his age, she said. But in a year or two his cock will fall off.

Now it was my turn to laugh—I couldn't help myself. I thought we were having a solemn moment.

A penance, I said.

Yes, she said, not hearing or understanding me. A pittance. I didn't correct her. The Pirate of Pittance, I said.

Upstairs, the carp fizzed in oil as we walked through the door, the pong of raw fish neutralized by hot canola and steam from the potatoes. The others had started to decorate the tree with foil stars, walnuts, shined apples. Aron circled the boughs with a box of wrapped chocolates. He passed me one the shape of a windmill and tugged my sleeve to demonstrate where I should place it. Behind him, Basia dispensed the tinsel in clumps, which Hania discreetly redistributed. A tin turtle presided near the top of the tree beside a crystal bauble. They hung the ornament with concentration, Basia cupping her palms around the figure in case it dropped. It occurred to me for the first time that the name of their pet, Baron, amalgamated those of the two children.

Where was the broken china, I wanted to know. The sherry glasses winging across the table. Would that come later? Would they arrive with the drunk or chronically medicated in-laws? At the very least, a cat should take down the Christmas tree. I sat on the edge of the sofa, moved by the tenderness with which they interacted, little Aron picking tinsel out of his sister's hair, and yet, for the first time I felt homesick. Homesick for where I couldn't discern—I hadn't returned to Detroit for two years, and didn't wish to. I didn't miss Arthur's family either—his coke-addled brother and sister-in-law who spent so much time on their Amalfi yacht their skin veritably crackled when they kissed your cheek. Nor did I miss their equine, translucent daughters who asked questions such as, *Daddy, does 'Lego' have a silent 't' like 'merlot'?* And yet, watching these perfect children speak to their perfect parents, and even their aunt, I felt like the ghost of Christmas dysfunction, their words incomprehensible to me not because I did not speak Polish, but because I did not speak this language of contentment, and suddenly I felt aware of *Christmas* as this other dimension occurring around me, which I could see, yet no more access than I could walk through a mirror. I noted this fact as you note a foot fallen asleep in a business meeting, where you can't stand up and shake your leg without making a scene. And so *Christmas* orbited around me. Little Basia spotted the first star from the living room window, which made Aron cry, until she conceded they had seen the star at same time, and we sat at the table, set with one extra place in case a homeless person arrived. I laughed and said, Isn't that me?

Dawid looked stricken, said, No, no. I emptied my glass of plum vodka and excused myself for the bathroom. I had every intent of going, but I stepped into the playroom instead.

The turtle dozed on his pile of rocks in the aquarium, his limbs unfurled to absorb light from the UV lamp, streaks of yellow highlighting his throat. I wanted to touch him. And then I was, my finger tracing a plate of the mosaic that formed his carapace. And then I was lifting him from the rocks and cradling his cool body against my breast. His limbs and neck snapped back inside the shell, which was not unlike our bones, I thought, if our ribs and spine fused together. His head had retracted, but I could see his mouth and eyes in the sphincter of his ancient throat muscles, like he was giving birth to himself. And then I was walking with Baron back into the hall, as I still had to go to the bathroom, and I didn't want to release him yet. Basia stood in the corridor, arms folded over her corduroy jumper.

Mom says we're breaking the wafer soon, she said, in hesitant American English I had no idea she knew.

Of course. Just saying hello to Baron.

She watched me carefully for a moment. I half expected her to shout for her mother, in that default kids have when an incident appears over their head.

Instead, she said, He likes cucumber, do you want to see? Okay.

She reached and I surrendered the tiny dinosaur into her arms, spotting my hands around his shell as she had for the decoration. She gave me a funny look.

In the kitchen, she set Baron on the counter while she removed a wand of cucumber from the refrigerator. She sliced a disc with a knife that looked heavy for her hands. When I realized this I skipped forward and said, Let me do that, but she had already severed a wet uneven edge. She hovered the segment in front of Baron's neck-hole.

Everything all right? Hania called from the dining room.
Coming, I said.

The girl and I watched in silence as Baron nudged his head
from the shell and nibbled the vegetable from her fingers.

That's brilliant, Basia. But I think your family misses us.
Why don't we put Baron back in the aquarium.

I shifted my weight and bounced as I said this, to trick my
bladder, to tell it to just hang on a second.

He's not finished.

Ok—let him finish and put him back. I'll go to the bathroom. Last one at the table is a rotten egg.

She gave me another funny look—possibly that expression
did not translate—and I lunged into the hallway.

She was sitting at the table when I returned, apologetically,
explaining I had something caught in my teeth. They didn't
mind—were filling the glasses with lemon water. When we
were seated, Dawid presented a wafer with a nativity scene
embossed on the front. He broke a piece, and passed the
cracker to his wife, who broke a piece, and passed it to me.
To prove what a joker I could be, I exclaimed: An apparition
of the Virgin Mary! They laughed charitably. Hania presented
the twelve dishes—fried carp; beetroot soup, thinner than
the Russian borscht I'd tried, but pleasant; pierogis; herrings
in cream, which I sampled to be polite; sauerkraut. I smiled
conspiringly at Aron, who had seen me trade my herring
for Basia's sauerkraut. In fairness, I took his sauerkraut too.
There were poppy seeds between his teeth when he grinned.
Gradually, perhaps with digestion, my spirit re-absorbed into
my body—the kids were cute; I'd missed pierogies, I ate
them all the time in Detroit; Lidia argued with her sister
about the cabbage rolls, which she had been in charge of; the
room swayed warmly; the kids opened their mouths at each
other, potato pancake gummed to their teeth. Before dinner,
I'd asked Lidia to help compose an obscene text message in
Polish—it involved idioms for "horse dick," and "you fuck
hedgehogs." But I thought now I would not send it. If he
wanted to talk, he knew where I lived. Still, I liked the idea
of Art copying the text into Google Translate, frowning at
the yield: *horse overhang*? I saved a draft just in case.

We had shared one pleasant Christmas together. The year before last, both of us jet-lagged from a week in Eastern Time—Arthur in Toronto for meetings, me visiting my mom and step-dad in Detroit. We landed back at Heathrow three o'clock on Christmas Day. Neither of us had made dinner reservations, and even if we wanted to cook, no shops were open. We went for a walk, to scavenge. We didn't pass a soul in the park, not even a dog-walker—on Piccadilly you could stroll down the middle of the road. And we did. Then we strolled down the middle of Regent Street, the city unfamiliar from the traffic lanes. We found a shop selling kebabs and ate in Trafalgar, our shadows spilling onto the steps of the National Gallery, the only shadows in London, gesturing to the moon, the purpling sky, neither of us desiring to speak, our mouths working the pita in silence. Later, we travelled home as we came, by the centers of roads, veering for the odd black taxi, our tongues oily with onion and lamb. We didn't talk until we re-entered our garden and familiar sounds called us back—the chirp of the alarm, Radio 2 in the kitchen, the washing machine. Then Arthur fetched wine from the cellar and I lit candles in the sitting room and we made love on the plush, boring carpet.

After Wigilia dinner, I stayed home while the others attended midnight mass. I had the idea I might wash the dishes, which we had left mounded on the table with the hollowed carp and bowls of pickles. I poured more plum vodka in the kitchen and turned to run the taps. That's when I saw Baron. Suspended in a pot of hot fat. Hania had transferred the fry oil to the sink, and the turtle now hung in its stillness, claws extended for the lip of the pot, long neck outstretched, eyes swollen shut, limbs yellowed and crisping—not fried, the oil had cooled down, but the skin flaked like dandruff—his ancient mouth clasped shut. I released a shuddering scream and dropped the vodka and staggered into the butcher block. I continued to judder backward until I found myself on the living room sofa, breathing heavily between my knees. I should have returned him to the aquarium myself—what was I thinking?—entrusting that task to a seven-year-old. I sat this way for a long time, temples beating into my thighbones, the air scratching my lungs.

Eventually, I calmed down enough to light one of Dawid's cigarettes. I smoked out the window, considering the silence of the street, which was muffled by a film of snow. I felt sick to my stomach, and this converged with a general homesickness, a nausea for time rather than space, I realized—missing the past, my life before. Across the road, a woman stood on her windowsill and re-enforced her curtain with spun cotton. As she stretched, I could see the tan pantyhose that sucked around her calves, her floury knees. Our eyes met. I flicked the cigarette onto the street and shut the window. I placed a lid over the oil in the kitchen, so they would not discover him that way, and lit a candle. My phone lit up. *Merry Christmas*, the message read, though it must have been Boxing Day in Thailand. The wax smelled of ginger. I turned on the radio and listened to the rustling Polish voices until the family came home.

Detail

A. E. Kulze

She hadn't meant to be cruel. Jack knew that. She wanted to crack him open. She wanted to get close to the part of him she could not see. Clem was sitting on the edge of the bed in only her underwear, her hair down and unadorned, her spine like a string of desert hills outside of Kandahar. She had said it casually, almost sensually, her chin on her shoulder and her eyes cast down at his body on the bed: "How many of those guys have you popped?" It was as if she thought it would arouse him to disclose a detail so intimate and dark. Jack was lying on his back on top of the covers, still in his uniform and socks, his boots stinking and flung to the floor. He stayed silent, swallowed, as he had been trained to do whenever he felt disturbed. He would not tell her, but a self-ish part of him wanted to see what would happen if he did. Clem waited a few seconds then retreated. "I'm sorry," she said. "You don't have to answer that."

She lay down beside him and put her ear to his heart, and as she listened Jack thought of Fifty-Six, an overweight man splayed out in the dirt, his belly open like a half-eaten cake. He thought of Fifty-Five and Fifty-Four, young men buckled inside a smoldering sedan. He thought mainly of their bodies, how easily they broke. Sometimes it amazed him that he had a body too.

*   *   *

It had been two years since Clem became pregnant with their first child and Jack agreed to take the job. The Air Force was desperate for RPA squadrons, and the position allowed him to serve domestically, to battle overseas from the comfort of a Georgia base. He could make things burn and smell no smoke, feel no heat. He could make things crumple from a distance of 12,000 miles and still return each night to his wife and child. He wrecked and loved. Wrecked and loved. Sometimes he could not keep them separate.

Jack and his squadron spent nearly all their time in a room they called "The Crate." The Crate was a detached cockpit about the size of a shipping container. It was sealed, apart from a tiny slit of a window, like a cell for solitary confinement. The difference was that it was full of servers and monitors and wires and joysticks for them to play with. Well not play with, exactly. Terms like that were burrs beneath the Commander's saddle. "This isn't a game," he liked to say whenever anyone appeared too relaxed. "I'm not giving you shits any prizes."

Jack was the sensor operator, the pilot's right hand man. The boys liked to joke that it was because he was sensitive, but he knew it was really because he was precise. He controlled the target. Laser. Camera. He saw the world in measurements of degrees. He was the eyes of the entire system—looking down on the jagged relief of a city, or a city block, or even just a single home, the laundry drying in its barren courtyard. He watched over, and at times he felt omniscient, wielding fate from 15,000 feet.

*   *   *

Jack arrived at the base to receive a new assignment. He was grateful. He hoped that the fresh orders and the images they led to would work to clear his head. In the morning, Clem had grown weepy over his silence the evening before, claiming he'd grown cold and aloof, which he knew to be true. Jack had found her in the tub, whimpering while clumsily snacking on Goldfish. As her hands shook a few of the crackers had fallen and become bloated with bathwater, and he felt at fault for the whole thing. On days like this he would observe his monitor closely hoping something colorful would distract him. But such gifts—a woman furiously working a goat teat until the milk came flowing, children playing marbles with the knucklebones of sheep—were rare. Most of the time Jack felt the urge to retreat, though to where he did not know.

For his last assignment he had been tasked with surveying a home in a remote village. It was a lifeless place, barely distinguishable from the dusty ground it rose up from. There had been little movement apart from the changing shape of a sheep herd and its teenage herder. There had been no visitors. There had only been suspicion, and at times Jack felt as if the Commander was just giving him something to do. His new watch, however, was high-value. The threat could become imminent. The target was hot. The drowsiness he felt dissipated like fog at dawn.

Jack oriented himself at his station, pulling his seatback upright so that he wouldn't slouch from an urge to sleep. His one-year-old had cried through the night with a cold, and he and Clem had taken turns suctioning the mucus from her tiny nose. He smelled of her, of moisture gone sour, of a softness he felt he did not deserve.

Jack received his coordinates and found himself peering over a network of buildings on the outskirts of a Pashtun town. It looked as if someone had dropped a pile of stones in a sandbox and a few scattered away from where the bulk of them had landed. Each building seemed as if it were built at a different time from the others, and with a different intention. The largest one was square-shaped and painted white, and the others were all gray and incongruous, like the poorly drawn shapes he imagined his child would one day scrawl. Surrounding the complex was a high mud wall, the roofs different gradients of tin.

Jack had recently moved into a new house. It was his family's first real home, and it looked like all of the other homes surrounding it. He decided that he could benefit from some physical distance between family life and work, so he and Clem chose a new development just a few miles from the base in what had once been a forest of longleaf pines. There was a small park for children and a manmade pond filled with snapping turtles, algae, and disappointing fish. It was a neighborhood for model American families, and the houses lined up as if in military formation. Each stood tall and straight, their differences only discernable by a coat of paint or the effort one put into the greenery. Clem had insisted on a buttery yellow, a color she had recently discovered to be a symbol of joy, optimism and fun. The choice made Jack feel fraudulent, as if he had signed a contract with stipulations he knew he could not meet.

On his screen he observed two small figures milling between the buildings and sagebrush growing in scattered clumps. As for the living, there was little else. He was reminded of how much Clem would hate it there, where few things grew, of how she believed "gardening put her in touch with what mattered." He did not know what that meant.

Clem had a way with flowers and shrubs. She treated them almost like children. She spent the last month of her pregnancy raking mulch into neat beds and coaxing rosebushes and germaniums until they bloomed. One day Jack found her still toiling away in the yard when he returned from his shift on the base. He stalled in the street just to watch her. He thought of the things you can learn about a person by observing them when they are alone. She was on her knees, packing dirt into a pedestal around some young plant, her round belly brushing the ground. The length of her brown hair was pulled back into an old scrunchie, and the shorter pieces stuck to the sweat on her cheeks. Jack lit a cigarette he had been storing in his glove compartment and watched her as she leaned into the branches of a lemon tree and stood there smelling it for some time. When she came out he could tell that she had been crying by the way she wiped her cheeks. She cried often, blaming it on hormones, but it had begun to make Jack angry. He figured it selfish that she believed she had the license to weep so freely. Days before he had watched a woman calmly collect her husband's fingers from the dirt, blowing on them as if they were dusty figurines. She had not cried and neither had he, even with the knowledge that the mess—all of it—had been his to clean.

*　*　*

It was early evening in the desert and the third day of Jack's new watch. Three young boys outside the main wall were hurling pebbles at a pack of dogs. Each time a pebble landed the dogs dispersed, before coming back together again to lick and bite one another.

The mission monitor told Jack that the order was to keep close watch for the rest of the week. The target was a man Intelligence had been searching for for some time. He was a senior adviser to the network, one head of a polycephalic snake. The hope was to cut them off one by one until the body was left to blindly wriggle about. Jack's job was to go in quick, lay the axe down fast, and get out before anything bites.

The sun had begun its descent over the landscape on his screen, and he watched as every element burned beneath the orange. The three boys were being called in by a woman's hand, which flapped erratically like a spooked bird. It reminded Jack of how his own mother would summon him in for dinner from the woods behind their home. He remembered how shattering it was. How the sound of his name was the first sign that his break from reality had not been won. How the enemy he had imagined would suddenly materialize into a forest of trees, the war hero into a small boy, and the grenade on the ground into the prickly fist of a pinecone. And then, that waving hand, moving as if to lure the entire outdoors back into the house, marked the end of it all.

Jack felt for the boys and watched as they walked back toward the compound entrance, their heads hanging down and their feet kicking up the stones and trash along their path. They entered beneath the woman's arm as she held the scrap metal gateway open, and together, raced toward the larger building for what Jack assumed would be a meal of rice and fruit and meat. The rest of his shift was the still, black sight of a place asleep.

Jack caught up with Laura then, the RPA's pilot and the unit's only woman. Laura was an outspoken redhead with severe green eyes and in her second trimester with twins. Some of the boys still called her "Angel" from the time when she was a legend in an F-16, but motherhood had since clipped her wings. Fortunately for Jack, the Air Force could still use her prowess on the ground. He liked having her around. She understood their job in ways he could not. She could say "bastard" instead of "target." She maintained a child's tidy sense of good and evil, her body built around an inflexible, Irish Catholic will.

She flew and fought with the center of herself, which she could feel even through a small sea of amniotic fluid. The Commander liked to use her as an example with the new recruits. He called her "living proof that modern warfare still requires old-fashioned skills." Or as Laura liked to say, "They can call them unmanned all they like, but there's always going to be some cat like me behind the wheel."

The two of them were sitting side-by-side in vinyl seats that looked like they belonged on a commercial jet. Laura spoke without turning to face him. "So there's talk of a shift swap."

"For who?" Jack asked. The rumor made him nervous. He often felt as if routine was the only thing that kept him from flying off.

"You and me. They want us on our guy during desert daylight."

"Really? So you mean we're night shift then?"

"That's what it sounds like." Jack felt heavy. He thought of Clem and the child asleep in the house alone. He thought of the windows, open to let in the breeze, and the flimsiness of the screens.

"Well is that going to be okay for you? I mean with the babies?" Jack said, trying to shift the weight of his own concern.

"Well it better be. Anyway, I figure it'll be nice to have the bed to myself all day while Chris is at work. I mean

I'm basically three people now," she said, rubbing the bulge beneath her flight suit. "And you've got it made too bud. No more sleepless nights with that baby."

"I guess," Jack said, astonished by her optimism. He envied her, but he also knew that hopefulness was impossible to hold. With each strike he watched it slip between his fingers.

Up until then he had been blessed with a normal father's workweek, returning home at six like a man who wore a tie. It had been a courtesy paid to him by the Commander, or rather, a courtesy paid to his wife, who had made a point of sending him their birth announcement. Clem wanted Jack to know what it was like to calm a crying child in the dead of the night and to lay her back down as serene as a stone. She wanted this, and she wanted Jack there for herself, to feel his hard body at her back on the nights she could not sleep.

The next day Jack received word of the shift change. The Commander told him he was on midnight to ten a.m. He claimed that Jack's skills were being wasted watching a dangerous man while he dreams, and Jack knew exactly what he meant. He wanted Jack to get know his target. He wanted Jack to see him live his days. He wanted him to watch as he and his boys gathered hay from a landscape of dried brush.

*   *   *

That evening Jack returned home to find Clem running a mop across the laminate flooring. She cleaned compulsively because the accomplishment of it made her feel better. She planned to start a landscaping business as soon as the child was old enough to go to school, but until then, she decided to test drive the life of her own mother, maintaining a clean household as if that alone could keep her sane.

"Clem-de-la-creme," Jack said from an entry mat that read Aloha! in letters shaped like bamboo.

Clem looked up and smiled half-heartedly, and he could tell the day had been hard. She had dotted concealer beneath her eyes but forgotten to rub it in.

"I ruined my thumbs today," she said. She leaned the mop against the wall and held them out for him to see, two bony nubs, the nail beds raw and pink as poultry.

"She's been wounded!" Jack cried out, trying to make light of the situation. He took the thumbs in his hands and kissed them.

"Thank you, Captain," Clem said, retrieving the chewed ends and tucking them into her fists. "Good thing you got here before I moved onto the others."

"Was it the baby?" he said.

"I don't know. But I guess her being sick could have gotten my nerves going."

"Anything else?" Jack asked. He wondered if it was him, if she had begun to realize that she was depending on a man who made rubble out of homes to hold theirs together. He wondered if she mourned him. Or maybe she just felt stupid. He imagined her pulling on the ends of her hair. *How could you be so stupid! Christ, Clem! He's fucked! Just watch the news!*

"I don't know," she said, returning to the mop and running it over a spot she had already cleaned. "It's like I suddenly wake up somewhere strange after sleeping the whole ride there."

Jack looked across the room to his child who was lying on her stomach inside of a mesh playpen. He walked up to it and found her teething on the ears of a rubber bunny that Clem had named Pollyanna, after the real one she had as a girl. She also had a black pig named Hamlet, a rooster named Lancelot, and an entire coop of chickens, though he knew none of their names. She was the daughter of a third generation farmer from upstate South Carolina. Or had been. He killed himself the year she graduated from high school, a single shot muffled through a goose down pillow. Jack met her shortly after it happened, when she had just entered the anger phase. "It was the pesticides," she had said over and over. "They gave him headaches. They made his eyes look red and insane." Jack held her hand through the rest of her mourning. He squeezed it, rubbed it. He watched it go limp when she fell asleep in his arms. This was how they fell in love. On one particularly dark day, he picked her up and promised he would never drop her.

Jack reached his hands down into the pen and scooped up

his daughter. He held her high above his head and looked into her eyes. Like distant planets, they called for curiosity and speculation. He could not tell what lay behind them, and he wondered what she would eventually be capable of, if it would shock him. As a boy, he used to bring home dead birds with the intention of burying them, but he could not recall the look on his mother's face.

In one of the books that Clem purchased to prepare for the arrival of the child, it made clear that the first year of her life would be the most critical. It is during this time, the book read, that bonding must occur. This sets the stage for the child to enter healthy relationships with other people and to appropriately experience and express a full range of emotions. This was something Jack wished he had never bothered to learn. Of course, bonding seems like the natural thing to do with one's child, but once he read this, it began to feel like a task they'd have to consciously execute. That left the possibility for failure, which was always on his mind.

"She's feeling better today," Clem said. "No more green snot."

"Great," said Jack, remembering how jarring it was when the awful color first came dripping from her nose. Clem had gone white, while Jack grew heavy with a guilt he had never felt before. It was only a sinus infection, the doctor assured them, something easily alleviated with a mild antibiotic, but there were still questions he couldn't shake. Where had the ugliness come from? And was he the one to invite it?

Jack waited until he and Clem were lying in bed to tell her about the shift change. She told him it was cowardly to casually whisper something like that in the dark. He knew it, but had done so anyway, fearing the concern on his face would say more than he meant to. He wanted to pass it off as harmless when he knew it was a descent, a sinker tied to his hip. It pulled him farther away, from civilians, their buoyant hopes. He felt horrible leaving her up there, clinging to some faulty lifeboat, thinking God, the great navigator, would ultimately save them both. "My mom thought that cold sheets were the worst part of sleeping alone," Clem said in the quiet before sleep. "But she managed somehow. After dad checked out she would put hot water bottles on his side of the bed so it still felt warm."

*   *   *

On the first day of his new schedule, Jack saw the target for the first time. He was a tall man. His strides were long enough to warrant recognition, like the mechanics of a newly patented machine. A turban sat atop his head in a nest of white cloth, and he wore loose, brown pants beneath a matching tunic and scarf. Jack watched him move across the complex toward the kitchen and duck his head to clear the entrance. At points like this he allowed his imagination to fill in the gaps. He envisioned a great many children sitting on a large ornately patterned rug. Pewter dishes of steaming rice and flat breads and apricots and eggs. Wives spooning out rations. He imagined the target sitting central to it all, mediating chaos and driving his teeth into stone fruits, the juice accumulating in crystals along his bearded chin.

A half hour later he emerged in the courtyard with some of the smaller children—one hanging from either arm. He put them down in the center of the yard beside a few toppled and rusted toy cars, which they drove through the dirt with their hands and tossed to the sky in mock explosions. The target entered the building where he had spent his morning, coming outside only once during the rest of Jack's shift. During the ten minutes he stood under the sun, Jack observed him closely, and it surprised him that a man so thin, with shoulders so slumped, could be so dangerous. Exhaustion appeared to be his principle quality, a symptom of a side note in his Intelligence folder, which said he was a father of twelve.

*   *   *

The following day Jack was let off early. At four a.m., a point in time which is neither night nor day, when the streets and houses and people lying in them are the closest they can be to dead. Little was happening in the desert on account of the extreme heat, so Jack was told to take advantage and get some rest. The base was slow, and when he walked toward his car in the nearly empty parking lot, swarms of palmetto bugs scurried beneath the shadow of his feet. Jack watched as they desperately beetled between the blackness and the bright of a streetlight to avoid the crush of his boots, and he thought about the wonder of a life lived on impulse, without a thing to love or grieve.

He drove the back roads home, which was just a mile farther than the regular way, but it took him past skeletons of empty farm stands and a Southern Baptist church. The church itself was nothing special, just a one-room cinderblock building with a plastic steeple attached to the roof, but it was the sign that he really wanted to see. Everyday it said something new in plastic lettering. Things like: There is no greater grace than forgiveness or With one's eyes squinted, take it all as a blessing. Jack liked to pretend that the messages were meant for him alone, as if some anonymous mentor had put them there to keep him in line. That day's lesson, lit up by two spotlights nestled in the flowerbed beneath: Cum inside Jesus. Somebody had rearranged the letters, and Jack was surprised to find himself struck by a sharp pang of sadness. He imagined some hopeless person discovering it the next morning, the kind of person who had turned to God as a last resort, or the deacon, who likely spent a portion of his day carefully deciding what it should say. Jack parked his car in the grass on the side of the road, stepped out, and walked toward the sign. A pile of letters had been left like litter among the pansies. He tried to decipher what it had read originally, but the exercise made him weary. His mind had grown too weak for games, so he decided to simplify. He popped off the letters one by one until Jesus was all that was there. He left it like that, a loaded name alone in the night.

At home, he moved carefully through his child's room as one would through a minefield, each step made in fear of setting something off. He leaned over the railing of her crib and found himself frozen there. A warm breeze rushed through the window, giving life to the mobile of origami cranes that hung over her head. Jack pushed his hand against the screen to check its strength, before reaching down and running his fingers against her cheeks. She squealed as if in response to a private conversation, and Jack wondered what the world had begun whispering in her ear.

He entered his own bedroom to find Clem curled up on one side of the bed. She was so close to the edge that one small shift could have made her fall. He undressed and climbed in and pulled her toward him so that the curve of her butt was tight against his groin. She did not wake, so he began to tell her in whispers. He would warm her up with a voice in her dreams. "Fifty-Six, sweet Clem. Fifty-Six. There will be more. I promise I don't enjoy it, but we all do things we don't enjoy. Once I—," he stopped. He wondered how much of the truth she could swallow before she choked, even while dreaming. He tired to sleep. He buried his face in her hair and sent himself into an empty space—a place in the mind as calm and cool and dark as the desert after sundown.

*   *   *

The next night the previous shift reported that the target had risen early and left the compound. He sped away on a motorbike and entered a home two towns over where he remained. Jack settled into his station and found the camera looking over a large clay and stone home, the motorbike parked along the street outside. Three hundred feet away a market stood out in a silent commotion of color.

Around mid-morning desert time, the target walked out of the home with a woman in a robin's egg colored burqa at his side. Jack could observe nothing of her apart from how the draping fabric moved as she walked or how the wind tried to take it away. The target mounted the bike and motioned for her climb on. She hesitated before seating herself sidesaddle, her head tilted against his back and her arms clutching at his chest as if he was all she had.

Jack pulled his view outward to follow the two as they roved through the disparate landscape, across sandy hills and irrigated pastures. He was reminded of his wedding day. He and Clem had driven away on a moped with ribbons and empty beer cans tied to the back, and he had felt so confident as she clung to him, so capable of taking care. He wondered if he would ever be that way again, like the target, motoring onward, staring resolutely ahead. Jack watched as the woman huddled even tighter against him, her garments flying like flames.

*   *   *

He found the woman alone the next morning. She was pacing the perimeter of the courtyard, her features exposed beneath a stormy-colored headscarf. Impulsively he pulled in tighter, a simple shift of the wrist, the joystick driven forward. His hope was to catch the color of her eyes, but he knew he could not get close enough. They remained as a nondescript as stones settled in sand. It was technological shortcoming, but at times Jack felt its limitations were intentional. Closeness could be cause for intimacy, and intimacy could be cause for failure. An ocular pigment, say, pistachio or soil, the lima bean shape of lips—those were things he could hold in his head. But a distant figure remained elusive and always out of reach. He stays remote. She stays obfuscated. Empathy is a lost vessel, unable to moor.

Intelligence told Jack the woman was the target's young bride, a third wife bred of a contract between himself and her father who had been associates for some time. She wandered the grounds of her new home as one would in a store full of intricate, breakable things. She ran her hand lightly down the back of a sinewy donkey tied to a post and brushed her fingers along a sheet strung up on a line. It was rare that Jack got to observe a woman he did not know, solitary, in meditation, and it made him feel heedless—something like stomping on flowers.

He looked away, down, toward the pimento cheese sandwich wedged between his thighs. Clem had packed it in a coat of cellophane and sliced into neat, loving little squares as one would for a child. Jack was not hungry, but he decided to use it as a diversion. He chewed the sandwich dutifully as he did most things, the bread and cheese and reduced-fat mayo sliding in lumps down his throat. He thought of Clem, of her gnawed fingers pressing into the bread, of the butter knife quivering. They always moved unsteadily, fervently, as if she was loading a gun.

Something about women began to seem enviable to him. They seemed so full of subtle feeling, of a need for feeling, so poised for the absurd task of being human. Jack remembered a girl, no older than ten, the only other female he had observed in length alone. She was the daughter of portly a Imam his squadron had hoped to engage, a man high up on their list. Jack had surveyed her home for two months during his first year, before he had a child of his own. The girl spent most of her time by herself in the central courtyard, fingering the potted plants that grew there or scrubbing dishes in the outdoor sink. She was always lively in spite of her loneliness, whirling from one wall to the other, her flitting hands like a pair of fat moths. Jack had wondered if that was what a daughter was—brimming, buoyant, an antidote to the ugly.

His comrade killed her one day, unintentionally. She was asleep when the house crumbled at the shock of a missile that took out her father and his van some fifty feet away. Jack threw up in his mouth when he heard, but he made himself put it back down before anyone noticed. I didn't do it, he told himself once, then twice, then always. At least there's that.

*   *   *

Within a week of the new wife's arrival things in The Crate had grown tense. The desert was hot with activity and hustle, and Jack sensed the anxiety that preceded a call to engage. Out of translation—log after log of recorded phone calls and faces seen where they shouldn't have been and fear fear fear—pieces of a plot began emerging. Jack decided that it was all very archeological. They dig and dig until they hit something hard. Uncover the fragments and see where they fit into the whole. Then uproot it. Study it. Start to feel small.

"They're talking about taking this guy out soon," Laura said through a yawn. Her eyes looked heavy, and the skin beneath them was colored like the peel of a plum. It was late and nearly the end of the week and both of them were feeling hazy. The whites of Jack's own eyes, Laura told him, looked veiny and red. "Like you've been crying," she said. The target was now under a 24-hour watch after his name was tied to a truck bomb that killed local police. Intelligence was uncovering his laurels, and his file grew larger by the day.

"I think it's a safe bet," she continued. "It's just a shame he's got like a million kids."

"They all do," Jack said, turning to his monitor.

The new wife was outside with two of the older girls who were close in age. She walked between them placing pinches of bread in her mouth, which she tore from the loaf end in her hand. The daughters listened on as she spoke through her chewing. About what, Jack could not know, but he imagined it to be some form of wisdom dispensing. When he is gone, fool yourself by placing a hot water bottle on his side of the bed.

Laura began sucking from the straw of a 7-Eleven Big Gulp settled on her stomach. "God they must get hot in all that damn fabric," she said between sips. "But I bet they make for some awesome maternity clothes. The things I would do to be able to wear a sheet."

Jack pulled back the camera and found the town to be drowning in a wash of midday sun. A white SUV entered his frame of sight. It was speeding—70, maybe 80, miles per hour, and its tires were coughing up great breaths of loose sand. Laura started yelling. "Shit!" she said grasping the joystick. "Shit. Shit. Pull in!"

Jack came in quick and stalked the vehicle. It drove recklessly across a makeshift road, veering to one side and then back again. He made the call to Intelligence and reported the pertinent facts: White SUV. One red door on the driver's side. Three passengers. Two in front. One in back. All haji. No visible weapons. Headed for target compound. They radioed back confirming their eyes were on it too and told him to keep the view tight. It's essential, they said, to get all three visuals. We need to see their faces.

The driver slowed down in a rush as the car approached the home, skidding out in front of the entry gate. The individual in back climbed out and banged his fist against the salvaged tin, and one of the sons came running to open it. Hearing the commotion, the Commander entered the Crate, and Jack could sense the heft of him standing behind his right shoulder. He rested his arm on the back of Jack's seat and leaned down, his breath drowning Jack's ear. "Keep tight on this," he whispered like Jack's father once did as they hid beneath the cover of a deer blind. "Keep tight."

Together, the son and the man from the car began prying open the gate, each pulling one side as the SUV passed through. Once it was parked, the other men emerged. The driver was wearing a jacket that was the same distinct green as Jack's own uniform. He also wore sunglasses, which would have been a point of frustration for Intelligence if he didn't wear them all the time. His name was known and catalogued, his identity and whereabouts chopped into the clean blocks of a spreadsheet. Some in their unit had even taken to calling him "Stevie Wonder" on account of his sporty looking shades. The belief was that he was hiding some kind of physical fault, like a lazy eye or the curdled milk look of an advanced cataract.

The target came out of a building on the left, along with one of the wives. She sent the son who met the men off toward the kitchen building as the target clasped their hands in his. He led the men inside, just as two of the other wives filed out from the kitchen across the way, each covered head to toe. Their hands were heavy with trays bearing things to eat and drink, and Jack tried to pick out the girl until another figure emerged slightly behind. One of her hands grasped the handle of a pitcher and the other supported the bottom, and she was trying to catch up without spilling anything over the edge. Jack wondered what would happen to her once the target was taken out, if she would imagine a face like his—pale and bald—as something to blame.

*   *   *

The following morning Jack learned that the men stayed past sunset and slipped away in the dark. They headed south toward the outskirts of the capital where the other shift took them out. "Apparently they had a perfect shot when the car pulled over and—I swear I'm not making this up—one guy got out to pee," Laura said. "It was some rookie sensor op's first. Three at a time. I heard he got a little wacked out over it."

"Really?" Jack said instinctively, though he didn't doubt it at all.

"Oh yeah. The Commander says he went completely stone faced."

Jack realized then that he had no idea what expression he wore after he pressed the button, and he wondered what people had seen in his face. Would he recognize himself if he saw it? Or would it be a haunting introduction? Meet you, the man you no longer know.

"Did they expect him to be smiling?" Jack asked.

Laura shrugged. "Anyway, they made him get a psych eval just to be safe, though I'm sure he'll be fine. They wouldn't have given him the job if they knew he couldn't handle it."

They did the same for Jack the first time he took a guy down. They made him an appointment with a older woman who had such an airy voice that it threatened to put him asleep. To stay awake he focused on picking the pills of fabric off the cushion of her worn couch, a cheap piece of furniture inhabited only by the unsound and screwed. She had been blunt, despite her cotton demeanor: "Sometimes you have to bite the bullet." But only Jack caught the pun.

*   *   *

When the Commander finally asked him to do it, Clem was aware even without Jack telling her because he tended to eat a little less during these times. He asked for one roll instead of two. He pushed peas and carrots over to the edge of his plate. He dreamt more than usual. He dreamt that he showed up late and failed various high school exams, or that his childhood dentist had removed all of his teeth. He went to replace the stale pack of cigarettes in his glove compartment and found a small orange bottle of Clem's alprazolam in its place, one blue pill left inside. He wasn't sure if she put it there while he slept or if it had it always been there, forgotten by him and her, waiting like an airbag to envelop an unhinged head. Every time he wondered if the next guy would be one too many, but then he'd realize that the answer never actually mattered. Either way he would wake up in the afternoon, dreary, his hands in fists. This is what war is, he thought, things will happen and you won't be able to stop them.

Window of opportunity was the phrase of the moment. Jack had to wait until their world invited him in. He sat stiffly at his station and tried hard not to take his eyes off the screen. He would take a sip from a Styrofoam cup of coffee and set it down without shifting his gaze. Beside him, Laura did her best to lighten the mood. "I wish we could take a detour over my mother-in-law's house," she said. "I'd love to send a Hellfire straight into her china collection." Jack tried for a genuine laugh, but it came out sounding closer to a cough. He was thinking of the girl, his girls, of how an impact like that would rattle their perfect bones.

He turned to a bird's eye view of the compound, where not a single soul had come outside. They'd seen no one since the target received the news about his friends two days prior. A courier had come in the morning to deliver the message, which the target had taken with a flat face and a small child in his arms, just outside of the kitchen doorway. He looked up then, as if to see what the sky was holding, and for a minute Jack wanted to wave.

They waited days for the family's fear to fade, and it did, slowly, like a bruise. After a week the young wife and an elder boy were the first to emerge. They came from the kitchen with a bucket of melon rinds to feed the sheep and goats that had exhausted their supply of hay. He filled a trough with water as she dumped the scraps out onto the ground, scratching behind their ears as they bent down to eat.

It is so easy, Jack thought, just to care for things.

*   *   *

When the target first appeared, he came out with two small children held in either hand. They crossed the yard and entered a building on the opposite side, and in the evening the three emerged again and walked back toward the kitchen.

When they reached the center of the yard one child broke off and ran ahead. The target mounted the other on his shoulders and moved slowly with the sun, his hands tight around the bones of her ankles.

Another week and pressure from the top had peaked, anticipation becoming its own kind of hell. Jack began to feel ragged, picked at like something left to rot in the street, so when the target finally came for air alone, he sensed the smallest bit of relief. He stood a few feet from the kitchen entrance as if to welcome a guest, and through it Jack imagined a crowd of pretty faces peering out. He looked clean and rested, his robes freshly pressed. Dearest Clem, meet Fifty-Seven. Things will happen.

The Commander stood behind him eating chips from a small bag and from his mouth Jack could hear the sound of things breaking. He told Jack what he already knew. Jack looked toward Laura seated at her station on his right, and he could tell she'd grown nervous. She was rotating her engagement ring with her thumb so that the diamond spun around and around her finger. Jack looked down at his hand clutched around the joystick control and felt fortunate that it was not shaking. At the sound of an order, he gave birth to a sea of dust and smoke. He watched its soft waves roll across his screen, and as he did he thought of the new word toying with his child's tongue. *Stop*, she had cried for days. *Stop. Stop. Stop.* She couldn't say it once. She hit Jack with it over and over, like a skipping stone. It was funny sometimes. When the neighbor's dog licked lavender soap residue off her little legs. *Stop!* But mostly it was unnerving. Like he was hurting her and he didn't know how or why.

Alkali Lake

Katie Young Foster

Eva tethered her granddaughters to two trees on the banks of Alkali Lake. She fastened the eleven-year-old to an ash tree, and the ten-year-old to an elm. Eva knotted the ropes to each girl's waist, leaving one hundred and fifty feet of play between girl and tree so they could walk with her onto the ice. She had considered leaving the girls in the truck while she fished, but Eva knew they wouldn't stay put. Ever since Lauren and Kathy's unexpected arrival on her doorstep over a week ago, Eva had been struggling to keep the girls off her heels; they didn't like to be left alone.

The ropes would keep her granddaughters in line, though Eva had sold it to them as a matter of safety. The winter was mild for this far north of North Platte, Nebraska. The drifts along the ridgeline were already melting. If either girl fell through the ice, Eva would use the rope to haul her out from shore. But Eva wasn't all that worried—ice fishing was safest the morning after a freeze, and it was barely eleven a.m. The truck's rear window was still coated with frost.

Eva and her granddaughters stood on Alkali's southern bank next to the frozen water. Lauren, the eleven-year-old, licked the ends of her limp blond hair. She was lanky, imprecisely long, her legs too skinny for her snowsuit. The fabric hung off her knees in rolls. Eva tugged on the rope at her grand-daughter's waist, testing the knot. Lauren made swimming motions with her hands. Her nose was broken in two places.

"Just double-checking," Eva said. She pulled on the rope again, this time to check that the knot at the base of the ash tree was secure.

Eva knelt to inspect Kathy's rope next. Her youngest grand-daughter was dark-haired and plump, with freckles that were red enough to be acne. A black ski mask covered her face. Only Kathy's eyes and chapped lips were visible through the slits in the fabric.

"It's like we're on leashes," Lauren said. She scratched Kathy behind the ears. Kathy barked, pretending to snap at fleas. "The trees are taking us for a walk."

Eva rolled her eyes and prayed the fish would be biting; she was due for a good catch. All of her usual signs of good luck were there—the bright sun, the dead field mouse grimed to the truck tire, sumac growing so thick it stained the shore. A hawk wheeled across the sky, and Eva wished it a silent *hello*. She had begun thinking of this first trip to Alkali as a trial run toward something more permanent. *Hand her the pliers when she asked? Notice when the wind changed directions?* Eva knew she shouldn't think of their time together in this way, but she was a superstitious woman. It was the season for perch. Any catfish they caught would be thrown into the trees, bad luck.

A burst of powder fell from the treetops, speckling their shoulders. Eva brushed the snow off her coat. She handed Kathy a baggie of ham. Kathy placed the bag between her teeth and stowed her hands in her pockets. The baggie dangled from Kathy's mouth at an angle, bumping against her chin. The ski mask and the ham made Eva think of an armed robber.

Eva took a deep breath, forcing her judgments to pass. Criticizing children was a trait Eva suffered—and had suf-fered from—since an early age. Her mother had been the same. *Bold as brass, too boyish, not enough flour in the biscuit mix*—Eva could remember all manner of faultfinding. Paula, her daughter, had come along years after Eva had expected to ever bear children. Eva had vowed to raise her with a lighter hand. But when Paula reached high school, Eva was almost sixty. By then, a familiar tone had crept into her parenting. *Boy hungry. Glitter crazy. Paula, the wild child.* Archie was more patient. *Sweet as pie,* he called their daughter, even when she ran away, returned, fled again. Even when she got pregnant at eighteen. When she cooked meth on their uninsured boat. *Sweet as pie.*

Eva shivered and tucked her fishing rod under one arm. She passed the rusted blue tackle box to Lauren.

"It's too heavy," Lauren said. "I don't want to carry it."

"The tackle box weighs five pounds," Eva said. "That's not much."

Lauren pulled down her pants and squatted to pee in the snow.

"Jesus," Eva said. First snooping, now this. She needed to start keeping a closer eye on Lauren. Just this morning she'd found Lauren in her bedroom, searching for mittens in the drawer that held Archie's old clothes. When Eva told her to look in the closet instead, Lauren had abruptly backed away, acting sly, as if she didn't want the help after all. Sullen girls both, Eva thought, but she hadn't raised them.

"Keep close," Eva said. "The ice is six inches or so, but the sun—it's bright today."

"Where's *your* leash?" Lauren asked, twisting the rope on her waist.

"Don't need one," Eva said. The lake's patterns were as familiar to her as the rise and fall of Archie's chest, or the twitch of his mustache moments before he sneezed. Archie, dead two years next week. Eva stepped onto ice the color of wet newspaper. The days had passed without him, somehow. She widened her stance and glanced at the bubbles and grit layered into the freeze. A beady minnow's eye glinted near her boot, frozen in the ice. The lake was egg-shaped, about two hundred yards across. There were no trees on the opposite shore—only grass, bent where deer had bedded down the night before. Eva spotted half a dozen abandoned fishing holes drilled into the ice. No one else was on the lake, at least that Eva could see. Most of the fishermen would arrive later in the day.

She thought about tossing her hat into the air, just like Archie used to when he first arrived at Alkali to fish. He'd holler, "I'm back, ladies!" before kissing Eva on the mouth— for luck, he'd say. Eva started across the lake, letting the girls sort themselves out. She wasn't going to baby them.

Lauren and Kathy took to the ice. Eva heard someone sliding, a thud. Laughter. She grinned but didn't turn around. She pictured Lauren army-crawling after her. Kathy would be following her older sister, more careful on the ice, panting, the ham still dangling from her mouth.

Weren't they all right, those girls? Eva shouldered her fishing pole. It was a question that had bobbed in and out of her mind all week. On Sunday, the girls' first night at her house, Eva had fed Lauren and Kathy fish and green beans and waited for them to tell her what had happened. Both girls avoided identifying the rail-thin man who had dropped them off at Eva's front door. She wanted to ask about the red balloon tattoo on the man's neck but instinct told her, *quiet.* Eva tried to phone Paula. The number was disconnected. She dialed again and listened to the error message. *I'm sorry, the party you are trying to reach is not available. Please hang up and try again.* She hadn't spoken to her daughter in a long time. Where did Paula live anymore? The girls wouldn't say. They lingered at the dining room table, lethargic until the early hours of the morning, when Eva heard them in the living room, moving around at last, watching a documentary on whales.

The next day she canceled her plans to eat at the Senior Center. She had arranged to take Ted and Jenny arrowhead hunting on the Radon Ranch that afternoon, but phoned to postpone. Jenny offered to send over some clothes for Lauren and Kathy. The choir would organize a potluck, she promised.

The girls slept late on that second day. Lauren was the first to wake up. Eva fed her oatmeal with raisins. They listened to the radio in silence. Eventually, Kathy trailed into the kitchen, yawning and clutching her pillow. Eva pulled the family album out of the boot closet and sat the girls down on the couch. Kathy collapsed next to her and leaned her head against Eva's shoulder. Lauren lay across the back spine of the sofa, feet dangling over the newspaper basket. She poked Eva in the back of the neck.

"Who's that?" Lauren asked.

"Your mom," Eva said, unsticking a photo from the page. The baby was smiling, drooling, wrapped in an afghan. She handed the photo to Lauren. "Your granddad, Archie, is the man holding her. You probably don't remember him. Look at his cowboy hat. That color of red was stylish back then, can you believe it?"

Eva turned to the back of the album. Two pictures, carefully laminated, were displayed on separate pages. On the left, a three-week-old Lauren, bald, cooing, naked except for a diaper. Eva—a younger, thinner Eva—was holding her up for the camera. On the right, newborn Kathy, dark-haired, solemn, tucked her pudgy fists under her chin.

"That's me," Kathy said, pointing.

"You look like a slug," Lauren said.

"I got to hold you four times," Eva told Lauren. She patted Kathy's knee. "But you, only once."

Lauren slithered off the couch and climbed onto the coffee table. Eva eyed Lauren's bare feet—was this how eleven-year-olds acted?—but held her tongue. Lauren lifted the photograph of Archie and baby Paula toward the ceiling. She folded the picture in half. Lauren brought the crease to her mouth and bit down. She started to chew on the photo.

Eva stood and yanked the picture out of Lauren's mouth. She unfolded and smoothed it out. A half-moon of teeth marks dotted baby Paula's face.

"Why'd you do a dumb thing like that?" Eva demanded.

"I'm not telling you," Lauren said. She lowered her voice. "I'm not telling you anything."

She ran out of the room. On the couch, Kathy sobbed over the bent photograph of Archie and Paula. Eva was at a loss. She dialed Paula's number, hoping she had called the wrong number before. *I'm sorry, the party you . . .*

"Grampy," Kathy said. "Grampy."

"You should be crying about your mom," Eva snapped. "Not Grampy." She ushered Kathy into her bedroom and sat her granddaughter down on the bed. She grabbed some deer jerky from her dresser drawer and an old photo of Archie in his waders, fishing at Alkali Lake. She handed both items to Kathy to calm her down.

"Look, there he is again," Eva said, nodding at the photograph. "Same old Grampy."

Kathy gnawed on a piece of jerky and lay down on the bed, peering at the picture of Archie. "He has a mustache in this one," she said, tearfully.

"I have more pictures of your mom, too," Eva offered, but Kathy didn't reply.

Eva found Lauren in the guest room, hiding under a sleeping bag. She couldn't tell if Lauren was crying, or just mad. She eased onto the bed and patted the girl's lumpy form.

"It's okay, the photo's okay," she said. "Don't worry about it."

"I'm not," Lauren said.

Eva reclined to show Lauren she was not going anywhere. The silence stretched around them, holding the room in thrall. A dozen mounted fish covered the walls. The bedspread and sheets were camouflage. Eva had had plans to build a display case in the guest room for Archie's arrowhead collection, but as she looked around, she realized there wouldn't be space for the girls if she did.

Her eyes drifted shut. What would she do with five hundred arrowheads if she didn't display them? Keep them in boxes under her bed? When Eva opened her eyes again, Lauren was snuggled into her side, snoring a little. The sleeping bag was bunched at the end of the bed, covering Kathy, who had snuck into the room and was now curled at her feet. Outside, the sun was partway up the sky—ten o'clock, maybe eleven. The trinkets on the windowsill had been rearranged. Arrowheads, Archie's chess pieces, a gorilla figurine—all were positioned in a new place on the sill, or missing. The girls must have been playing last night, she figured. Eva glanced down at Lauren beside her. When asleep, and snoring, Lauren sounded just like Paula.

The week continued, faster than Eva could have predicted, a series of peaks and plunges. During the daylight hours, the girls were mopey, lethargic half-children. They wandered aimlessly room to room, trailing Eva as she swept, and washed dishes, and fixed the zipper on her coat. At night, Lauren and Kathy unraveled. They fought and screamed and threw ceramic mugs. They shredded Eva's bank statements and wrote cuss words on the guest room walls. Both girls seemed younger than their ages when the sun went down. Eva flip-flopped between admiring this nighttime version of her granddaughters and thinking how much better it would be for them if they could manage their emotions. They'd come to her home lacking almost everything: toothbrushes, training bras, the wherewithal to bait a line. Eva didn't know who to blame for their lack of refinement—Paula, or herself.

On their fifth day together, Eva drove the girls to the market. They wandered the aisles and helped her hunt down groceries. Back home, she found a bar of lavender soap in Lauren's coat pocket. They drove back to the store to return it and apologize to the manager. Eva's cheeks were still burning when they emerged and started across the parking lot. Lauren sucked on the end of her ponytail, her face expressionless. Kathy was crying, distraught, and halfway across the lot, she bolted in front of a slow-moving car. Eva yelled out. The car honked and stopped, and Kathy rushed back to Eva and crushed her ribs with a shaky embrace. Eva stopped yelling and hugged her back, and Lauren, too. They swayed in the parking lot for almost five minutes. Over the girls' heads, Eva spotted a cardinal on the hood of a parked Volkswagen Beetle. She felt an inexplicable sense of relief. Birds were omens, she believed, bringers of fortune. Change was coming. It had to be, Eva thought. Back home, she lit a series of lemon-scented candles and pocketed her special deer hoof, hoping to encourage good luck.

At midnight on the sixth night of the girls' visit, Eva called Ted, a friend from choir. She had to shout over Kathy's wails and Lauren's monotonous banging of her fork on the table to ask Ted to search for Paula's listing on the Internet. Maybe her daughter would crop up online. Eva tapped her foot in a surge of hope, waiting for Ted to start up his Mac. Maybe Paula was sobering up, would visit soon. Ted searched websites and social media for twenty minutes—nothing.

"We're going ice fishing," Eva announced, hanging up the phone. Her hands were shaking. She'd slept two hours the night before. Maybe the ice would wear the girls out, make them sleep until sunup. Maybe one more week—two weeks, three—wasn't impossible if they liked to fish as much as she did, as much as Archie. "Let's see what the lake makes of you."

A small hand gripped the back of Eva's coat. Kathy had caught up to her, had hurried across the ice to accompany her to the abandoned fishing holes. Eva took a deep breath and pulled Kathy along behind her. "Yee-haw," Kathy said, giggling, the bag of ham still clamped between her teeth. Eva glanced back to check on her oldest granddaughter's progress. Lauren was trailing behind, running a few steps and sliding, the tackle box acting as a counterweight to balance any sudden slip or fall. The girls' ropes snaked across the ice.

Eva reached the abandoned fishing holes first. She looked at the girls' ropes weaving across the ice behind them; they still had some slack. Kathy loosened her grip on Eva's coat. Eva squatted and scooped slush from one of the holes. The sun's reflection glinted on the open water. Eva shielded her eyes.

"Is it a jelly fish?" Kathy asked. She poked at a nearby bubble that was captured in the freeze. The girl knelt and put her teeth on the ice and tried to gnaw.

"Just air caught," Eva said, hooking a worm from her pocket to use as bait. The worm would freeze in a matter of minutes. Anyway, it was already dead. "Stop it. You'll chip something."

"Can I help you fish, Grandma?" Kathy asked.

"Spit in the hole first," Eva said. She set the line and bobber. She'd only brought one fishing pole, intending they could share. "It's tradition."

Lauren joined her sister at the ice-fishing hole. The girls took turns spitting until a bubbly film had collected along the sides of the ice. At Eva's nod, Kathy opened the baggie and sprinkled in globules of ham, another tradition. Eva spit, too. Within moments the red bobber dipped under.

"Bingo!" Eva shouted, reeling frantically. A blurry shape appeared in the mouth of the hole. Eva loosened the line and the girls chased the fish's shadow like a pair of cats, touching the places where the gray silhouette glided beneath their fingers. With a tug that brought a soft splash, Eva swung the perch out of the hole, into the air. She flipped it away from the girls.

"Pliers," Eva said, but neither granddaughter moved. They were watching the perch slap against the ice, their mouths opening and closing, making sucking noises. They were mimicking the fish. Determined not to be disappointed by their slow uptake, Eva rummaged around in the toolbox for the needle-nose pliers and dug out the imbedded hook from the perch's mouth. The worm was gone. Eva crouched and, groaning a bit because of her knee, bashed the fish against the lake until it was still. She pulled a knife from the pocket of her overalls and cut the fish's belly open and held it out to the girls, cold blood dripping down her fingers and into the sleeves of her coat. Eva used her index finger to clear the guts from the perch's belly. Innards spilled onto the ice.

"Pick something," Eva said, grabbing the dime-sized heart for herself. "Your granddad and I—we always did this."

"Gross," Lauren said.

"I'll do it, Grandma," Kathy said. She leaned across Eva's shoulder and pointed to the jellied sac of yellow flecks.

"Eggs," Eva said. "Archie's favorite too. They're all yours, Kitty-cat."

Kathy peeled off her mittens and picked up an egg between her thumb and pointer finger. It slid away and plopped to the ground. Lauren deliberated for several moments before rolling her eyes and choosing a tiny rib bone. She crunched the bone between her teeth. After watching Lauren swallow, Kathy scooped up the egg again and nibbled. She began to gag.

"Okay," Eva said, almost with relief. She sent up a luck-prayer and swallowed the fish heart whole. "Now we can start." They had the whole afternoon ahead of them—hours before sundown. Eva tore off a piece of the perch's flesh to bait her next line. She dropped the bobber into the hole they had prepared with spit. She left the fish carcass piled to the side. Watching the line, Eva felt like a bear in one of those kid's books Paula used to read—hunched over, poised, waiting for the smallest change in the water's surface. The girls waited, too.

"What about that one?" Lauren said. She pointed to a lone ice-fishing hole twenty-five feet in the direction from which they had walked. Lauren had been watching it closely for a while now.

"That's yours," Eva said quickly. In the summertime, when Alkali's waterline was at its lowest, a sandbar appeared near that part of the lake. The sandbar could be anywhere from two to five feet below the ice during the winter months. It was not a good place to fish for perch—too shallow. One of the locals had made a mistake when positioning the ice auger, and had drilled a hole through the ice into the sand at the bottom of the lake. "Go play. I'll call you back if I need you."

"Play?"

"Yeah, play," Eva said. She stared at Lauren and remembered how Paula would cross her arms and glare in just that same way. "Well?" Eva said.

"I'm hungry," Lauren announced. She picked up her sister's rope. "We're taking the ham." Kathy was still on hands and knees, gagging, as Lauren pulled her across the ice. As she slid past, Kathy managed to snag the Ziploc baggie from the top of the tackle box and stuff it down her coat.

The girls' ropes crisscrossed as Lauren headed back toward the shore where they were tethered. Lauren dropped her hold on Kathy's rope and belly-slithered to the opening of the ice-fishing hole. She pushed up her coat sleeve and dipped her entire arm into the lake.

"Don't freeze that hand!" Eva called.

"Blah, blah!" Lauren yelled back. She pulled her arm out of the water and stuck her face in instead.

"You're kidding me," Eva said, under her breath. She glanced around. The day was windless, the weather above freezing—the water wouldn't harm Lauren's skin too much, she figured, as long as the girl used her sweater or coat to towel off.

Kathy was on her feet now, puny in Eva's old Carhartts, her face a black hole behind the mask. Kathy tapped Lauren on the shoulder over and over to get her sister's attention. The lake was empty, crystalline—sound carried clearly over the ice. Eva found herself listening to her granddaughters' conversation.

"We should go back over there with Grandma," Kathy was saying. Her pant legs were wet from sliding. She scuffed slush with her toe, and then leaned over to tap Lauren again.

Lauren pulled her face out of the water, slush dribbling down her chin. "No," she said, loud enough for Eva to hear.

"You're not going to tell her what happened?" Kathy asked.

"No," Lauren repeated. Again, she plunged her arm into the ice-fishing hole, into the water, as if trying to reach the bottom of the lake. "That lady is crazy."

"Who?" Kathy asked. "Mom or Grandma?"

"*Let nature be judge of that,*" Lauren said, in a voice Eva recognized as an imitation of her own. Kathy repeated the line back to her sister, and both girls started giggling. The phrase was something Eva had recited more times than she'd realized over the past week. Eva turned away to hide her annoyance. The words did sound ridiculous when Lauren spoke them out loud.

"Where're you at?" Eva said, speaking quietly so the girls couldn't hear. She hooked a perch—a ten-incher—and tossed it into the black trash bag she'd brought to carry home the catch. She had barely enough time to bait the line before hooking the next fish on her pole. She jerked fish after fish from the water. Lauren and Kathy fell silent. Eva managed to glance up for a moment—had it been minutes? hours?—and caught them sprawled on the ice, arms over faces. They were napping.

Eva snuck glances at the branches and the sky, looking for birds. She liked to think Archie could be reincarnated as a bird. A pelican, maybe, or a seagull. Her husband was the type of man who would wait to pass until she and Paula, too, could follow. After all, what had that man loved more than fishing, his wife, and his daughter? Maybe coffee, Eva figured, so about two years ago she'd started leaving day-old grounds in the compost pit. Eva felt silly whenever she dumped the coffee in the morning, but she kept an eye out for any birds that showed an interest, just in case.

Above the ridgeline, the sun grew yolky and ran out in all directions. Shadows from the trees stretched thin onto the ice. The warmest part of the day was leaving. At Eva's feet, small punches perforated the black plastic as the fish suffocated and stilled. She bent to check the thickness of the ice and caught a glimpse of her reflection. Her forehead was scratched and puffy from the cold. Eva remembered the girls—were they warm enough? She glanced across the lake. Lauren was awake, lying on her belly beside the ice-fishing hole, her hand in the water again.

"Careful what you pull out of there," Eva hollered, thinking about the many fishing hooks she and Archie had lost in Alkali over the years. Who knew when Lauren's last tetanus shot had been?

Eva felt a pull on the line. She reeled in a catfish, the first of the day. She stomped on its head with her cleats. On the far shore, a muskrat skittered across the ice and burrowed back into its den.

"Shit," Eva said. The afternoon's sun was almost gone, and her luck had run out—it was time to grab the girls and go home.

"Whoa!"

Eva glanced up in time to see Lauren pull her arm out of the lake, raising a fistful of reeds. The girl scrambled to her feet just as something lumpy and dark dropped from her palm onto the ice. Even from a distance, Eva recognized her lucky deer hoof. She kept the hoof in a box in Archie's underwear drawer, alongside his driver's license and last pack of cigarettes. Archie had given it to her after a hunt on the Radon Ranch. The deer had been a Boone and Crockett buck, an eight by five with drop tines on the right; she'd cooked chili from it for a good three years, the best years of her life. Paula had entered middle school and was thriving; Archie was alive and healthy.

"Look it here!" Lauren said. She tossed the hoof in the air and caught it, then tripped over the rope. She untangled herself and jogged over to Eva. She stopped in front of Eva's fishing hole, keeping the open water between them. Eva reached across the hole and touched the hoof's rubbery sole.

"Did your mom tell you to take this?" Eva said, quietly. Paula had known about the deer hoof, had always mocked its lucky properties. Eva was certain Lauren had stolen it from her bedroom. Maybe Kathy was in on it, too.

"No," Lauren said. "Take it? I found it in the lake. It was sunk into the sand at the bottom, close enough to reach."

"You put it in the water." Eva tried to keep her voice calm. She wanted to say: *It might not work now.*

"That's not true. It's mine. I found it." Lauren was defiant, her chin jutting out in a way that meant she wasn't going to cry. The girl stepped forward, across the hole, suddenly bold. The top of her head came up to Eva's shoulder. Neither granddaughter was very tall, or very strong. Eva wasn't afraid of them.

"Lauren found it, Grandma. I watched her," Kathy said, a few beats too late. Pieces of ham were stuck in her teeth.

"Are you going to keep lying to me?" Eva felt burdened by the children in front of her, who looked and acted like Paula but were not. She picked up the trash bag of fish and stood there, winded, unsure of what to do next. Should she ground Lauren? Demand the girls wait for her in the truck? Eva dropped the trash bag of fish. A dozen perch spun across the ice. Others slid into the ice-fishing hole and floated on the water's surface, dead. The girls backed away from Eva. The last of the sunset played along their faces, forming triangles of light. Both of the girls were squinting. The horizon behind them darkened.

"Get out of here," Eva said. She reeled in the line and left the fish alone. She drove the girls toward shore. "Get. We're leaving."

"I found it," Lauren said again. "I'm sorry, Grandma, I thought I found it." She dropped the deer hoof quickly, as if it burned. The hoof clacked against the ice.

A shadow drifted between Eva and the girls, barely visible. All three of them looked up. A hawk swung dark across the sky, heading south. The sight of the bird filled Eva with deep remorse. Eva picked up the deer hoof and clutched it in her hand.

"Why did you take this?" Eva asked again, but all the energy had left her.

The hawk turned unexpectedly and flew so low that Eva had to duck. It had sighted the hoard of fish. Lauren shrieked, lifted her hands to the rope on her waist. Both girls cowered. Eva could almost taste their fear as the last of the sunset drained from the lake.

The hawk swung abruptly into the trees, hunting something unseen. Darkness settled fully on the ice. Eva reached for the girls, heart pounding, remembering their nighttime patterns. Lauren struggled to untie the rope around her waist. Eva tried to stop her, but Lauren loosened the knot and darted across the lake, free, heading for shore. In the trees, Lauren paused to undo Kathy's rope from the elm.

"What are you doing?" Eva said. She tried to grab her youngest granddaughter, but Kathy bolted into the trees after her sister, starting up the chase. "Don't leave," Kathy cried. "Don't leave!" The trees rustled where the girl's body slipped through the branches.

Eva heard a crack like a gunshot and felt her body shift.

It took her a moment to realize she'd fallen through the ice. She shouted in surprise. In the confusion of the hawk and the girls, she had tread on a soft spot, or maybe the ice had been thin all along. Eva had one leg in the water, and the other foot on ice. Alkali Lake had swallowed her to the knee.

After a few moments the shock of the fall wore away. Her heartbeat slowed. Eva started toward shore, but as she put weight on the ice, her other foot fell through. The water was cold at first, but after awhile Eva could not feel it. She tried hoisting her leg, but the lake would not hold her. She began breaking a path with the heels of her boots, chipping away at the ice. The lake was shallow at the start, but grew deeper the closer she got to land. The sandbar, Eva remembered. She had fallen through the ice where the lake was too shallow to fish. Soon Eva was up to her waist in the water. She broke the ice with the hoof of the deer Archie had killed for her. When her hands became too numb to grip, she allowed the talisman to slip from her fingers. She used her fists to fracture the ice.

"Lauren," she said. "Kathy."

Someone was waiting for Eva on shore. The girl held up a rope. It was too dark to see which granddaughter had come back for her, too hard to see if the other was waiting in the skirts of the trees, or had fled.

Cough

Jonathan Durbin

At that time I lived downtown, and downtown was a mess. The military arranged my neighborhood into zones, cordoned streets off with Humvees and M-16s and concrete barricades. If I wanted to go out for food or rent a video—back then we still rented videos—I'd have to bring a phone bill with me to prove I lived where I said. The days were hazy with smoke, the nights febrile and restless. Everything smelled like a tire fire. I developed a terrible cough. I was coughing into the phone when I spoke to Natasha. She asked if I wanted to spend the weekend at her country house. We weren't getting along, but I agreed. I needed the fresh air, and it was too sad and strange to stay in my apartment alone.

We arrived at dusk. While Natasha piloted her hatchback into the barn, I waited on the porch with her dog Cody, an old German Shepherd with rheumy eyes and a gray muzzle. He didn't like me much, but he didn't put up a fight when she handed me the leash. The dog and I stood there beside each other, watching the car's taillights flicker, listening to its engine tick as it cooled in the September air.

For dinner Natasha made rabbit stew. Afterward we took Cody for a walk up by the road. We didn't see anyone. Not one car passed us by. Her nearest neighbor lived two miles away, or so she told me. Natasha liked the privacy of her country house. She used to say the place was a sanctuary from the noise and heat of the city, which sounds absurd now, but she really talked like that then. I thought she overstated her case. I'd been at her country house before and found its stillness suffocating. The hush there was a bad hush. But anything was better than downtown.

That evening the sky was midnight blue, the mountains in the distance darker against it. I remember it being quiet except for the throating of Indian-summer crickets and gravel crunching under our heels, and if there was conversation between us, I don't recall what was said. Once we returned to the house Natasha filled a bowl with water for Cody and invited me upstairs. She had a new king-size bed up there, plush with pillows and a white duvet. We had sex on it, but the mattress was too soft for purchase in our usual positions, so I took her from behind. It didn't last long. She fell asleep on top of the covers, and I went nude onto the balcony to stare in the direction of the road. I wish I could say I came to an understanding out there, but I didn't. I was only twenty-four, numb and a little ill, and mainly I spent that time trying not to cough.

In the morning she drove us to town for breakfast. We ate at a diner with other refugees from the city. I recognized a few of them from magazines and television. Everyone looked ashy, crestfallen. Some of them were crying right there at their tables. Natasha and I had fried eggs and bacon and listened to the cutlery click against our plates. The diner was playing music, but they'd turned the volume down low, and the music made the diner feel more somber than anything else. As if to apologize for that, a waitress bounced around the room taking orders, calling everyone Sugar or Honey. Natasha winced each time. After my second cup of coffee, hot and watery and thick with grit at the bottom, she said she wanted to leave. *I can't be in here anymore*, she told me.

Natasha held Cody's leash while we walked the town's main drag. We stopped at a candle store and a jewelry place but spent most of the morning in an antiques shop. The dust in there started me coughing again. Everything was dirty—tables and dressers, vintage travel posters and war medals, GI footlockers rusted shut and brown with age. I didn't want to buy anything, didn't have any money to spend, but I'd been coughing so hard that it felt rude not to take something home. I settled on a writing desk. I needed a desk in my apartment, even if it cost sixty dollars and was too small for me. I carried it back to the car, stifling coughs against its legs. Natasha loaded it into her trunk. I would have loaded it in myself, but she worried I'd cough and scratch the paint. Cody watched her struggle, his front paws up on the bumper. I told him to heel. The dog ignored me, scraping his nails against the metal.

When we got back to her house she tied Cody up in the yard and poured us a couple of whiskeys. We went to the sunroom to drink, and I must have had the idea that drinking would turn into fooling around. But just as we sat down on the couch, that's when her husband called. I knew it was Ed because she told me, covering the receiver with her palm. She crept off to the kitchen to speak with him in private. I couldn't hear the conversation because her voice was low and serious, but then her voice was always low and serious, so that didn't mean much. Ed worked as a venture capitalist. He was out west, in San Francisco, launching a startup. He hadn't been home in weeks, hadn't seen the disaster downtown, and kept calling her to check in. He wanted to know how Natasha was. *How do you think*? That's what she told me she told him, later that afternoon.

I drank my whiskey and drank hers too and paced the sunroom for half an hour. When I tired of pacing I went to the kitchen and came up behind Natasha. She was still on the phone and waved me off, but I held her hips and kissed her neck and soon enough she told him she had to go. She placed her hands flat on the fridge—feet shoulder-width apart, as if being frisked—while I slid down her jeans and rubbed her between the legs. We fell to the floor. The tile was cold but having sex there seemed like a good way to pass a few dead minutes that afternoon. Then she wanted to nap. We went upstairs and lay down. She slept with an arm thrown over my chest. I stared at the ceiling fan, waiting for the day to fade.

It was past seven when she woke and went to brush her teeth. While she was in the bathroom I pushed myself up on the mattress by my elbows and asked her what Ed thought about me. I knew what I was doing. As Natasha spat and ran the faucet, a cold sort of weightlessness ballooned in my chest. She came out of the bathroom still holding her toothbrush, gripping it in her fist like a knife, and asked if I was serious. Why would I bring him up? Was I trying to make everything worse? I didn't say anything to that, or if I did say something I didn't say it fast enough, because the next thing I knew she told me she'd prefer it if I slept on the couch downstairs. Next to the dog bed. She really said that: *next to the dog bed.* She was wearing a white tank top and purple panties with gold buckles at the sides. Those buckles were silly. We didn't eat dinner that night.

I went downstairs, where Cody was lying on the floor beside the couch. He gave me a slumped look, something like, *Oh, it's you.* I turned on the TV and he turned over and passed out, legs jittery, whimpering in his sleep. As usual, there was nothing to watch. Every channel showed the same footage on loop, the same footage over and over—the smoking horror downtown, the dust-coated soldiers patrolling it, the newscasters who all seemed to speak with the same muddy voice. I fell asleep while the mayor urged everyone to spend money and dreamed that I tried to buy groceries for Natasha but my credit cards kept being declined.

At dawn I woke to find her sitting on the couch by my feet, the TV droning on. I watched her watch downtown burn, and then I sat up, rubbed her back and said I was sorry. She said no, she was sorry. I told her not to apologize, but she said I didn't understand. She was right about that. I'd never been with a married woman before and didn't know which questions I wanted answered, never mind how to ask them. So I let Natasha talk. That seemed to help her mood. She told me that if she ever got divorced, she would keep the country house. The paperwork was in her name, and Cody needed the space. She'd brought the dog to her marriage, and she'd make sure to keep him if she left. Her apartment in the city was too small for a German Shepherd.

I kissed her cheek and she put her hand in my underwear and climbed on top of me. For a while we had slow, drained morning sex. In the middle of it she knelt between my legs and put me in her mouth. It still took me a long time to finish. Gray light from the TV leached the color from her hair, and between the sirens and the people shouting and crying downtown, I couldn't concentrate. At one point I tried to turn off the TV. I looked around for the remote and saw Cody sitting by the coffee table, watching us go at it with dull brown eyes.

Once it ended I drifted off again into a weird thin morning sleep, but coughed myself awake at seven and stumbled around the house looking for her. Natasha was in the kitchen brewing coffee. I told her how good it smelled, and she said she'd added cinnamon to the grounds. She offered me a crimped morning-after smile, then told me to shower. *Coffee'll be ready when you're out.* So I went upstairs and undressed in her bathroom, turning the spray on as hot as I could stand. I didn't like that shower. The water was hard country water and smelled like rust. No matter how much I soaped, I never left it feeling clean.

After drying myself I dressed and went back to the kitchen. I wanted coffee and to plan our day, but found Natasha hunched over the table, talking on her phone. She was louder than normal. While I got a mug and hunted for sweetener, I overheard more than I should have. I didn't mean to eavesdrop, but I didn't not mean to, either. It didn't take long to gather she was on with her husband again and he was saying things she didn't like. She kept asking him, *How do you know about him? But how do you know?* and when I poured my coffee my hand shook so much I spilled.

As I sopped up the mess with a paper towel, Natasha began to cry right there in the kitchen, right into her flip phone. She cried like this: *whef whef whef.* It was a soft and awful noise. That was the first time I'd seen her cry. I didn't know what to do. Should I have stroked her arm, told her everything would be all right? Or should I have gone for a walk so she could cry alone? I stood by the coffeemaker thinking those thoughts for so long that I caught the rest of her conversation. I wish

I'd let her be, but hindsight is twenty-twenty. I'm older now. I like to think I've learned a few things.

As it turned out, she and Ed were talking about some man, some friend of theirs who had gone missing. This missing man had been at work downtown the morning the city was attacked. Ed had just spoken to the man's wife over the phone, and then Ed called Natasha afterward to tell her how strange the man's wife had sounded. The wife had reason to sound strange: there had been a search for her husband, but now the search was over. The police had told her that he was presumed dead.

The wife decided to search by herself. She designed and printed out some missing-person posters. She'd tried to tack them to a wall downtown, but there were so many posters of other missing people already there that there wasn't any room. To put up even one she would have had to cover over someone else's poster, or else take it down. So she brought her posters home and poured herself some wine and drank until she got service—phones were spottier back then, switchboards always overloaded—and then she called Ed. She was drunk. On the west coast it had been four a.m. Ed was asleep and hadn't expected to pick up the phone and hear screaming.

Natasha talked and listened and wiped tears from her cheeks with the back of her hand. Before she hung up she told Ed she loved him. Once she was off the phone, I sat beside her and asked if there was anything I could do. She said no, sniffling, pushing the wet brown hair off her face, telling me that if we expected to eat dinner she'd have to drive to town for groceries. I said I'd be happy to come with, but she shook her head. Cody needed a walk. Could I take him? If I got hungry and she hadn't returned, there were eggs and milk in the fridge.

Cody and I watched her reverse the hatchback out of the barn, exhaust leaking from its tailpipe in loose gray wisps. I hooked the dog's leash to his collar and together we followed her car off the property. Natasha turned right toward town and I turned left, walking alongside the dog in the grassy ditch that ran parallel to the road. The sky was icy blue, the day clean and cool and tasting of spruce trees. I filled my chest with that taste and didn't cough once.

Cody spotted the birds before I did. Across the road, maybe a quarter mile up, a flock of them circled something on the ground, something hidden by a clump of reeds. The dog barked and strained on the leash. I held him back, but that only made him strain harder. His collar cut into his throat, and he began to choke. I tried to reason with him, told him to calm down, said we'd walk that way to see whatever it was those birds were circling, but he didn't listen. His hips quivered, and his tail stuck straight out, and he whined and coughed so much that I unhooked his leash and set him free. I laughed a little at how his paws scrabbled every which way over the pavement, as if he'd suddenly remembered how to be a younger dog. He bounded into the ditch on the other side of the road and disappeared from my view.

It took a few minutes for me to hike up to the reeds. At first when I parted them and saw that scene, I did a double take. An animal was lying there, bleeding out into the dirt. For a moment I thought it was Cody. My windpipe shrunk to the size of a wire. My breath whistled in my chest. But it wasn't Cody. It was a fawn—its hide wet, rear legs broken and askew, black lips pulled back into a sneer. Bloody mucous bubbled from its nose.

I don't know why I'd thought it was Cody, but that initial feeling was so strong that I had to touch the fawn with my bare hand to be certain I hadn't imagined things. Its little chest trembled under my palm, its wild black eye rolled in its socket. The fawn's forelegs twitched, as if it intended to run. Judging by the smashed look of its hindquarters, I thought it had been clipped by a car. Cody was nowhere to be seen.

I called for the dog, expecting him to shuffle out of a patch of dry grass with a baleful look, sulky because I'd ruined something else for him. But he didn't come. The only response I got was from the birds overhead—caws shot through with notes of panic, or maybe frustration. So I left the fawn dying there and wandered off to find Cody. I should have killed the animal to stop its suffering, I know, but I had no idea how. I guess I could have tried to break its neck, but I doubted I'd be able to crack its spine, even if I stepped on it.

I spent an hour trudging the fields out there, yelling Cody's name. On that side of the road, the ditch gave way to grassland that ended in forest, and I walked the tree line to see if I could spot him. Once or twice I thought I did, a gray shadow loping through the woods, but if it was him, he was faster than any twelve-year-old dog had a right to be. After a while I gave up and went to check the fields on the other side of the road. I passed the fawn again on my way. It hadn't died yet. It was so small. Blood matted its chin.

Cody wasn't on the other side of the road either. I searched for another twenty minutes, then doubled back toward the house. It was close to noon, and I figured Natasha would be home. I was thinking that if she came with me to look, the dog would show up, probably smirking when he did. But the barn was empty. No hatchback, no Natasha. I let myself into the house, poured a whiskey and sat in the sunroom, drinking and waiting. After my second glass I fell asleep. I woke in the late afternoon, the light hot and dry and pinning me to the couch. Natasha was unpacking groceries in the kitchen. A bottle of wine clinked to the counter, and there was a kiss of air when she opened the fridge.

I expected to anger her, to make her cry again, to hear her accuse me of negligence or worse, but I told her the whole story anyhow: the birds, the fawn, how I suspected it had been a hit-and-run, how I hoped the animal had died, how I believed Cody was hiding in the woods to punish us. It took me a while to get it out because I had a coughing fit in the middle of my telling. She shuddered—she denied it, but I knew my coughing bothered her—and that was when I thought she'd yell at me, really let it fly. Instead she grabbed her keys and pushed past me on her way to the door. I tied my sneakers and followed her up the driveway. We left the groceries on the counter, chilled slabs of tuna steak sitting in meltwater.

Her idea was to search both sides of the road at once. She took the side with the fawn and I stayed on the side with her country house. Ten minutes later I was ready to turn around. I couldn't stop coughing. The whiskey had dried to a film in my mouth, and passing out had swollen my sinuses. All of me ached. But I kept going, I didn't give in. When at last I saw her walking back across the road toward the house, face turned down to the pavement, I caught up to her and told her not to worry. Once he got hungry enough Cody would find his way home, that's what I said. Natasha gave me a bleary look.

By then it was near dusk. She seared the tuna while I salted and oiled some asparagus. The plan had been for us to barbecue and eat outside on her front porch. That didn't feel like the right move anymore, but we did it anyway. Both of us ate in silence, scanning the road for signs of the dog. It was a cloudy evening, and night fell fast. After we finished it was dark, full-on. I couldn't see anything past her porch light's resin-yellow glow, just a couple of fat moths flirting around.

While I rinsed our plates and glasses and loaded the dishwasher, Natasha went to the basement. She returned with two big plastic flashlights, the kind with lunchbox handles, and gave me one. Mine was weak and sputtered when I turned it on. I had to bang it against the kitchen counter to make it work. She winced. Hers worked fine.

We went back out, this time switching sides. Her beam flickered across the grass, stuttering every time she took a step. I swept mine across the fields in a more even way, lighting up the tree line. I really believed I'd find Cody. I thought I'd catch the reflection of his pupils first—blank animal eyes flashing at me from the forest—but I didn't. I didn't catch anything at all, just leaves and darkness veined with branches. It was another quiet night, no sound save for the crickets and our voices and wind rustling through the grass. Like earlier, Natasha would yell *Cody*, and then I'd yell *Cody*, too. We'd wait a minute or so and then repeat ourselves. If there were other animals in the woods, we scared them off.

Maybe a half hour in, I stumbled across the fawn. It was in the same position I'd found it that morning. It died with its ear pressed flat to its skull, black eye open and glaring at the sky, hide still slick, mouth open, teeth seething with ants. I touched its belly with my sneaker to make sure it was gone. That's when Natasha called for me. She was done for the night and headed back to the house. I rubbed my sneaker in the dirt to clean it and walked back to the road to meet her.

We placed our flashlights on the coffee table and drank some whiskey on her couch. For a while I held her hand, and then I used it to lead her upstairs. I undressed her, pulling her pants off by the ankles, lifting her shirt up over her head and unhooking her bra. She lay down while I took off my clothes and turned out the lights. Then I climbed into bed and held her from behind, my arm between her breasts. We had sex like that, but it was odd sex. Our timing was off. Nothing about it made sense. It was weak and empty and full of dread, and afterward she curled up on herself and her back hitched. *Whef whef whef.* Before passing out, I offered to help her make missing dog posters. Natasha had plenty of Cody photos, new and old. The last thing I remember before sleep was her calling me an asshole.

Around three I coughed myself awake. I wanted to apologize to her—tell her I'd take the couch if I was going to keep her up—but she was gone. Her side of the bed was empty, her pillow cool to the touch. I thought she might be looking for the dog again and got up to see if I was right. I shuffled to the balcony, imagining her beam skittering around out there, hearing her voice lilt on the wind.

Natasha wasn't in the fields. She didn't have a flashlight. She wore a bathrobe and paced her driveway, her heels black with dirt, as she spoke into her phone. I strained to hear her, then realized I didn't need to. She was louder than normal. She was talking to Ed. Who else would she call? Cody was his dog too.

But she wasn't telling him about Cody. She was as urgent and harsh as I'd ever heard her, clutching her robe shut and walking in frenzied circles, the bulb on the porch casting her in that thick yellow light. *Why did she call you? Why were you that person? Why won't you tell me why?* My eyes stung. I bit my lip. For the first time in a long time I felt for her, I really did. If I'd been able to put it into words, I would have liked to tell her how much. But my throat was sore, and my chest began to itch, and the only things I knew to say to her were meant to make her upset. A cough came on quicker than I could stifle it. I tried to kill it with a fist in my mouth, but it scraped itself out of me anyway, a wet noise that echoed in the dark.

Natasha stopped where she was. She glared at me, and for a moment we locked eyes. Then she shuddered and turned away. When she continued she raised her voice, I'm sure because she wanted me to hear what she said. *Don't worry. That was nothing. Just the wind. You know the wind up here.* I stayed on the balcony deciding what to do, watching her shake and listening to her shout questions, willing her to look at me again. Then, after a few more minutes of that, I climbed back into bed. She must have joined me later because we woke up together, plenty of white space between us.

The following morning we called the local shelter, the police, the state troopers. No one had seen a German Shepherd. Everyone she spoke with promised to alert Natasha if they did. She gave them her landlines in case they couldn't get through to her cell. They said they'd be in touch. They said they understood.

At noon we got into her car and she drove us back to the city. We spent that ride in silence and hardly said goodbye when we parted. She dropped me off at the subway station in Union Square and popped the trunk so I could take my writing desk. I struggled to carry it home, coughing the whole way. The subways were hazy. Everything underground smelled like burned rubber. To get past the barricade on my street I had to show my August bill to a soldier, a blond kid who looked seventeen and told me he couldn't believe how much I was paying Verizon.

I only spoke to Natasha over the phone three or four more times after that. We didn't see each other in person again. She never found Cody, at least not that I know. The dog disappeared. So did she, sort of. Natasha moved to San Francisco. I knew that because we exchanged emails for a while—on birthdays and holidays and other occasions. Last I heard, she'd remarried and had a couple of kids. I'd like to believe that she's doing well, wherever she is. I am. Not long after that weekend I rented a new apartment uptown. I got another job too, a better job, and started a retirement plan. I met girls my age and dated a few of them seriously. My cough went away. The military didn't stay in town much longer. I could walk around my neighborhood, phone-bill free. By December that year, the burning stopped and the smell mostly dissipated. Eventually downtown recovered, but it was never the same.

Communion

Jonathan Nehls

Manolo came around the garage and into the backyard, and there was the worker he hired, lying on the ground, facedown and motionless, his cheek resting on the concrete patio. At first Manolo didn't understand. He looked around the yard, squinting, screening the swirling dust from his eyes. The gutter had ripped free from the eave. The ladder had fallen, and now leaned away from the house against the fence. Below, and around the worker, roofing shingles were scattered. A hammer. A box of nails. The wind gusted and whistled through the gutter brackets where the gutter had broken free.

He stood there a while looking down at the worker. The boy's arm was contorted and pulled up above his head as if the arm had no bones at all. For a moment Manolo thought the boy lay so still he might just be sleeping, the only movement the wind working through his hair. Then Manolo noticed the puddle of urine. The swelling at the neck below the collar of the boy's flannel shirt. He could only think, Why? Why are you doing this? Stop it. *Get up*.

After a while he heard the worker gasp, a grating breath like a trashcan dragged across concrete. But Manolo didn't understand the sound. He confused it with the wind, the thrashing and howling. "Oye, nos vamos," he said and stepped to nudge the boy with his foot, but there was the puddle of urine.

"Oye . . . " he said, but he had forgotten the boy's name. He'd picked him up that morning on the corner of California and Park in Five Points, picked him from the other men who straggled about the corner, picked him out of pity. The boy looked like a cast off, his face slippery and flat as a cactus paddle. He had the goggle-eyed look of Raúl Velasco, but wore no glasses. Wide mouthed and thin lipped like a frog, with a shock of black hair that hung in flaps over his ears, and bangs sheared high up on his forehead. He smelled of campfire.

The boy had the accent of a chilango. That morning, the boy's voice trilled in Manolo's ears as they drove north to the work site in Thornton. It rose and fell and hung lazily at the end of each sentence. Manolo gritted his teeth at the sound. At first he thought it was a joke, an imitation. He'd only ever heard such accents in movies, or on TV, and always exaggerated, always mocked. Manolo had only worked with men from the north, Chihuahua, Durango, and never met anyone who spoke this way, almost couldn't believe it. He'd heard Sureños couldn't be trusted, that they were always scheming, waiting to take advantage of the simplest kindness, to make you look like a fool. When he glanced at the boy in the passenger seat, he couldn't help but think of the saying: haz patria, mata un chilango.

It wasn't till the boy stepped down from the truck that he knew he'd made a mistake: the boy wore cowboy boots. He watched the soles of the boots as the boy clambered up the ladder, and knew he'd have to come back and fix the work.

Manolo stood now, studying the boots wedged against the ground. He ran a hand down his face, and pressed a thumb and finger to his sockets to wipe away the tears. He thought about the body, what to do. Thought of police and deportation. The consequences resided in the back of his mind like cockroaches emerging in darkness to swarm and feed on his nerves. This same fear swelled to the surface when he'd see a cop or pass a wreck on the side of the road. One time he saw a car's hood in flames and a woman on the shoulder flailing her arms. He drove on. When his wife and son had first arrived, they took a drive up Clear Creek Canyon to Central City, and on their return, around a tight curve, they came upon car, mangled and high centered on a guardrail. He slowed, saw blood, an arm shoved through the windshield. He looked at his wife starting to cry, his son in her arms, and turned his focus to the road ahead.

* * *

Four years before, Manolo had never considered going north till his friend Edgar Mozo, who'd been away a few years, came home to Delicias. While Edgar was away he sent money, and his parents had built a second story and repainted their house and tiled the floors. They had a new truck and two television sets, while everyone else in the neighborhood had an ear to the radio, feet on the ground. Edgar convinced Manolo to come with him, offered to help pay for the trip, and guaranteed a job at the slaughterhouse in Greeley—Colorado Beef Solutions.

Manolo had just turned twenty-one and his wife was pregnant. He sold everything his wife didn't need—she moved in with her parents—and he and Edgar arrived in Greeley two weeks later. The whole town smelled of manure. Edgar swore he'd get used to it.

They worked together on the line, on the kill side of the plant, shoulder to shoulder, stripping hides. The air was fogged with steam and smelled of iron and manure, bleach and ammonia. It burned their eyes. All day the carcasses came swooping down, dangling from a chain, conveyed along a rail overhead. By the time the carcasses reached them, the legs were bare, and they carried on, skinning the flanks. They went back and forth between the knife—swiping it sharp—and the air saw. Their arms slicked with sweat, backs aching, hands throbbing. And then another and another, sometimes two hundred in an hour. The whole operation sounded like an auto shop, with the buzz of air saws and the hydraulic lifts and the knives scraping against sharpening rods.

At first, Manolo struggled to keep pace. He got tired, but never complained because no one would listen. There was one rule: the chain never stops. The supervisors stalked the line just waiting for it to stop. Everywhere their eyes scrutinized, appraised. He learned other rules that didn't need saying: Keep your mouth shut. Keep your head down. Do as you're told.

After a while, it seemed as if the blades had sprung from Manolo's own hands. After years, he could see it in the hands of others, fingers seized, hands clenching tools even when empty, the blades that made them whole.

Edgar had left out how hard it would be. Not just the work but the feeling of being watched, of being fenced in, like anyone they passed on the street could finger them and send them away. Everyone knew how they got there—Mexicans in a meatpacking town—whether they said it or not, and their knowing was a threat.

Manolo and Edgar lived with two other men in a one-room apartment within walking distance of the plant. They could never rid themselves of the smell in their skin and clothes, ammonia and fat, like potatoes gone slimy with rot. Their life was work, the scars of it, the smell of it. They hardly went out. Drank at home on the weekends. Fished the river. Watched American TV. The work bore on them and they sank, weary each day, but without fail, sick, injured or otherwise spent, they rose, put on their white pants and white shirts and white rubber boots, stuffed their white aprons and goggles into their white helmets, and headed off to the early shift at five a.m. That was why they wanted Mexicans, because they were reliable, didn't say a word, and there was always another in line. Manolo later found out he'd been recruited, and Edgar had earned a $150 dollar bonus.

Six months into his time at the plant, Manolo got a phone call from his wife. His first son was born. The men celebrated at a musty bar south of the plant along the railroad. The floors were greasy, the air buzzed with red neon light, and the smell somewhere of puke—even the bar smelled like work. After that, they went more often, a second job, they joked. More than once Manolo did something he'd never tell his wife. But eventually he grew tired of it. The guys gave him a hard time, told him to loosen up, live a little. After a year, he moved to a rented room with a toilet and sink.

There were all sorts of accidents: knives slipped, saws tore and ripped, chains and conveyor belts gripped and crushed. The injuries were mostly minor, but every now and then, someone would lose a finger or hand. He'd heard that years before, a man scorched his lungs breathing in too much bleach. No one was left unscathed: hands throbbed and blistered, joints grinded, disks slipped. Few could bear the piling on, much less for six dollars an hour. By then Manolo was already on his way out, thinking about how to bring his family, keeping an ear open for construction work in Denver.

Accidents were all the more likely when they pushed, when the chain moved too fast—and that was when it happened. Edgar worked beside him like most days, but he was spent, sweating out liquor. An hour in, Manolo heard the screech of an air saw cutting through bone, and looked down to see blood splattered on his apron. He turned and Edgar was holding his wrist, silent, staring at it. The saw had sheared up his hand and buried deep into his forearm. The wound looked like shredded raspberry Jell-O. The saw swung back and forth, dangling above from its hose. The blood came, streaming in a cord at Edgar's elbow and dribbling onto his white boots and through the steel grating to the floor below. Edgar's chin trembled and his stomach clenched. He looked at Manolo, holding out his wrist as if he wanted Manolo to take it, to admit it was real.

Manolo found a clean towel and wrapped Edgar's arm, while below, the supervisor gave them a look—*what's the hold up?*—and shoved a pointed finger toward the kill floor. Manolo held Edgar and guided him past the others, down the stairs. The chains clanked and the carcasses were conveyed onward. The saws buzzed again. The chain never stops.

Edgar offered the supervisor his arm. He took it and wrapped the towel and gripped it. "Hold it," he said, gripping the wrist. "Like this, hold it." But Edgar just panted and rubbed his chest with his good hand. A worker edged past them, carrying a bucket of bleach, and climbed the stairs. The supervisor nodded to Manolo, and flicked his chin at the stairs—*back to work.*

Plant doctors cleared Edgar for work within a week, his arm strapped to his chest in a sling, hand contorted in a gesture of begging. They had him spraying down cattle before they entered the chute and climbed what they called "The Stairway to Heaven." After that, Manolo rarely ran into Edgar, who drank more, his eyes swollen and rimmed with insolence. His roommates would hogtie him on occasion when he went berserk, flailing with broken bottles.

The company had it out for Edgar. He was an inconvenience. A worker who couldn't work, who more and more often showed up nearly drunk, who sulked and eyed everyone. He smirked at his superiors under the delusion that he was untouchable, that the accident would shield him. He slid as far as they let him. At the plant, a worker with a perfect record was on notice. Others recognized the double standard, contemplated the circumstances of their own injuries. Fellow workers came to resent him, Manolo included, called him radio viejo, because he didn't work. He was a vago with doctored papers who had a claw for a hand, and if inspectors came, an inconsistency would need explaining. They had to put him low, grind him down to nothing.

The last time Manolo saw Edgar was in a bathroom at work. Edgar sat on a chair—watching the bathroom, which was his job. He was talking to himself when Manolo came in. Manolo asked who he was talking to, and Edgar said, "Nadie." He looked around. "Nadie." Manolo looked him in the eyes but Edgar's glance evaded. His hand curled like a claw, tucked to his chest. When Manolo said goodbye, Edgar muttered and nodded as if chewing on tough meat. Manolo never saw him again. He'd heard rumors about amputation, that they ousted Edgar, deported him, sent him to a mental hospital. There was no word from him back home in Delicias. Manolo sent what he owed to Edgar's family, told them he'd keep an eye out for him. As far as anyone knew, he had just disappeared.

Manolo tried to justify his indifference, clear himself of guilt. Edgar was careless, had brought it on, ruined himself with drink. Edgar was cursed. What could Manolo have done? He had a wife and son to think about. If a man fell and you grabbed him, he would drag you down. The residue of failure, the taint, would stick to you. What sense did it make for him to stick out his neck?

A hundred times Manolo thought he'd seen him. Always on the side of the road, out of the corner of his eye like some spirit haunting him. Once, he was sure he had. It was in the same part of town where he'd picked up the boy. He had been in Denver a few years by that time. His wife had arrived with their son and another was on the way. He slowed and pulled to the curb where a man sat on the stairs of a boarded up warehouse. It was the middle of summer and hot, but the man wore a satin Dodgers jacket that was grimy, the shine worn off, and frayed at the elbows. The LA emblem over the heart, reminded Manolo of a canister vacuum. His jeans were oversized, and his black work boots, too, like boxes on his feet. He couldn't remember Edgar's face, but felt, somehow, it was him. Manolo asked if he needed work. The man pulled his hands from his pockets, whole, boney, sound, and gestured as if to cast him off. Manolo nodded and drove on.

He felt it coming, the trial, the judgment, the day he'd have to answer.

*   *   *

He couldn't help but think of Edgar as he looked at the boy, as if one had caused the other. The wind kicked up and howled. Leaves spun in the air and flattened against the fence along with trash bags and cardboard boxes. The yard was bare, no trees, sod on pallets yet to be laid.

And then all at once he heard. A low moan punctured by grunts and gasps. The boy huffed through his nostrils, coughed, meaning to say something, but nothing would come. Manolo knelt down and put his hand to the boy's back. He grunted and Manolo, spooked, fell back on his elbows. He scrambled on his hands and knees to the boy's face. The boy's eyes strained, screwed up, speaking.

"¿Estás bien?" Manolo said. He put his hand to the boy's head, brushed back his hair. There was swelling at his neck, but nothing to explain why the boy lay there like he did. He sat back on his haunches and panted. *Move.* He smacked the ground and whimpered. That something would move him. *Hijo de la chingada.*

He felt the urine soaking through the knees of his jeans. He stood and surveyed the yard. Of course there was no one. No one had seen anything. It was early fall, dusk descending, and with it, the wind biting cold, the sky graying, browning.

He went out to his truck. All the neighboring houses were empty and dark. Chipboard dumpsters sat in each driveway. No one had moved in yet. There was the show house, but the realtor had gone home. He backed the truck into the garage and closed the roll door. He opened the truck's passenger door and left it gaping and came out through the door to the backyard.

He squatted and put his hand on the boy's back, and brought the boy's arm down against his side. He considered for a moment and then did it, pulled at the boy's side till he lay face up. He weaved his hands under the boy's armpits, grabbed his own wrist and heaved, hugging the boy to his chest. His head lolled and fell into Manolo's face. The boy's hair in his mouth. The smell of campfire. He lugged the boy to the garage, his boots hissing over the concrete. The boy was heavy, limp, slippery like a trash bag full of Jell-O. At the truck he leaned back into the cab and hoisted the boy back into the seat. He sat the boy and buckled him, patted him on the knee. The boy's head drooped against his shoulder, all the while watching as Manolo backed out the driver's side.

He went to the backyard and kicked the shingles into a pile and gathered them up with the nails and the hammer and tossed it all in the truck bed. He struggled with the ladder against the wind, but mastered it, and strapped it to the truck rack.

*   *   *

He knew of only one hospital, St. Luke's, near where he'd picked up the boy downtown. As he started out, the boy seemed to watch him, a thread of drool running from the corner of his mouth. He nudged the boy's chin so he'd look out the window. Though every now and then, he nodded as if the boy were watching, assuring him, everything would be fine. He couldn't hear the boy breathing but saw his breath on the window, a fog that spread and shrunk.

Down I-25 the wind thudded against the truck, driving it into the adjoining lane. He saw in the rearview, a roof shingle lift and suck off into the darkness. Headlights appeared like eyes widened then shut. In the distance the city shone in a brown haze against the night sky. Cranes jutted up from towering concrete and steel cages.

He exited on the 23rd Street Viaduct. Below the South Platte and the vast bottomland was cast in darkness but for a bonfire that flickered against the walls of a vacant warehouse, and wafted out upon the rail yards. He continued on down Park Avenue. The boy hadn't moved or changed position, only rocked, now and then, jolted by a pothole or a turn, though Manolo drove warily.

When he neared the hospital, he had to double back, crossing through a parking lot, passing a demolished building, crooked rebar and mounds of concrete, before finally he saw EMERGENCY in red lights. The hospital had four wings, in the shape of an X, brick the color of a browning apple. He parked behind a berm of junipers and studied the entrance. A parked ambulance blocked his view. The idling engine filled the cab with a stream of hot air. He was sweating and trembling. When he looked to the boy, he found his hand on the boy's knee, and removed it and gripped the shifter. The boy's mouth gaped, his eye trained outside, somewhere.

After a while the ambulance drove off. A janitor stood at the entrance, smoking a cigarette. He dropped it on the ground and stomped it, and made to go in, but looked at his watch, and pulled out another. He smoked. He finished and swept up the cigarettes and pushed a trashcan through the doors. Manolo watched and waited. No one came. He pulled the truck into the roundabout and parked near the entrance. The lobby was clear but for the back of a few heads looking up at a TV, and a nurse behind a counter. He pulled up a ways more, so no one inside could see him. He surveyed the roundabout, the drive, and got out. Rounding the hood of the truck, he noticed a camera near the entrance. He turned, two more on pillars on either side of the drive. He placed his hand on the hood. He got back in the truck and drove on.

He tried to focus, driving and ducking, searching the entrances of the hospital, some place to leave the boy. He should have been home hours ago and thought about calling his wife, but what would he say? Everywhere he looked threatened detection. The parking lot glowed, and the few people walking there and along the street, if he unloaded the boy's body—there was nowhere. He slowed, nearing a parking garage. The booth was unmanned, the arm up. He turned in. He climbed and circled up the ramp and parked in a corner where it was dark.

His hand was on the boy's knee again. By now he'd realized the boy was injured beyond fixing. He should have said something human, but could only say, "Ya llegamos," as if they had both arrived at a place long before decided. He hadn't meant to do it like this, but he was already going through with it. He kept thinking there should be more to say.

The explanations, signing papers, somehow he'd be implicated, he'd be blamed. He'd be taken away, then his family, jailed and deported. He didn't know the boy. He knew the reek of campfire smoke and knew the boy was alone. If he had papers at all, they were fake like his own. Manolo had lived now four years answering to the name of a man who didn't exist.

He leaned over the steering wheel, his breath caught. He sobbed for a while but none of it went away. He wiped away the tears with a forearm and backed out.

Back on Park Avenue large stretches of the street were dark. He reached a corner where the darkness matted and blackened and seemed to have no end, and he drifted down it as if pulled by a current. He lurked, passing low brick buildings, loading docks and warehouses, vacant lots with tumble weeds wadded up against fences. The street was strewn with bottles, steel barrels, piles of tires. A car rusted to the bone, resting on its axles. Windows covered by metal lath or plywood, or smashed in. Walls rioted by graffiti. A continuous rumble of trains droned in the distance. He cut the lights and rolled on a few more blocks, coming to a stop alongside a lot overloaded with stacks of pallets. On the horizon a water tower stood black against the darkness, its roof caved in.

He nudged the truck along the lot and pulled into an alley. The wind, the distant howl of a train echoing, but no sound that would break the desolation.

He pulled the parking brake and got out, holding his chin to his chest for the wind. The boy slumped toward the door, and he undid the belt, and heaved him up as if shouldering a side of beef. He laid the boy down, and stood, inhaled the bad air, grains of dust in his teeth. The boy slumped against the fence.

*   *   *

A few days later, Manolo read the death notice in the newspaper. He'd arrived to work in darkness, hours early in each of the days *since*, and found the paper on the steps of a portable parked near a job site. The portable was an office and a kitchen and a locker-room, wood paneled and carpeted orange. A bulletin board of maps and blueprints hung on the wall, a lock box for keys. Each morning they gathered here and discussed assignments. He sat at a picnic table, slipped off the paper's rubber band, and wound it about a finger till it swelled. No one would come for another hour. He loosed the pages with the swollen finger. The police sketch was bad. The face triangular, a broad forehead that narrowed to a slight chin. The eyes dull and speechless. Only the mouth looked familiar, the lips flat and stretched like a rubber band. He folded the paper over, held it up like a shield, and scanned the article with dread. . . . *body abandoned . . . alive but unresponsive . . . blunt force head and neck trauma . . . severe brain damage . . . died 12 hours later during surgery . . . no identification . . . failed to identify the man . . . foul play a possibility.* He'd seen enough movies to imagine: stacks of stainless steel slabs, beds on casters, body bags tagged: *John Doe.* There would be no funeral. The boy's only relatives lived thousands of miles away in DF or Oaxaca or Chiapas. No one to claim the body, no one to identify it.

The roofing job was altogether forgotten; wind had torn

shingles off all the houses, hurled sheets of chipboard, splintered a few windows. The boy's death never came up. Never, even when he wanted it.

The dread graveled through his stomach and seared in his chest, burrowed in his heart and hardened. He carried the dread with him, gnarled around it. He worked obediently, guarded, tight-lipped, head down, more than reliable, like a man condemned, working penance. He came to an understanding: things happen for a reason. He cultivated a sense of destiny and swallowed the guilt, the needling suggestion of cowardice, however much it arose. His actions had provoked God. He gave up asking why, and like a child, accepted, *Porque sí.*

He felt dread at his sons' birthday parties, watching the swaying body of Spiderman or Buzz Lightyear hang from a tree, and the children below, sifting through the grass, rummaging its entrails. When no more candy could be found, the children turned their attention to the piñata itself, pulled it down, and dismembered it. One would tear apart the legs and put on the boots, another would poke out the eyes and wear the head as a mask. They'd run around the yard with their fists out, dressed in the remnants of another man.

He had kept the boy's possessions: a Velcro wallet, an orange Bic lighter, a comb, a single brass key, a pencil nearly worn to the lead with bite marks, the eraser gone, its clasp bit shut. The wallet contained slips of paper, scrawled with lists of names and numbers, a 5,000 peso note with the images of the Niños Héroes, seventeen dollars, a prayer card depicting San Judas Tadeo, a picture of a young girl, worn, the corners torn away as if it was once taped to a wall, and a label that read: DOBLE BUENA SUERTE. He kept it all in a box like a shrine, secret and sacred.

One morning, he found his boys in his bedroom, the contents of the box spread out on the bed. He stood in the doorway, panicked, breathing through his nostrils, rubbing his pant leg between finger and thumb, glared, but did not say a word, glared till the boys slunk from the room. He kept these objects so that someone might find them, that he would be obliged to explain, unburden himself. He had rifled the boy's pockets as he slumped against the fence, and taken his possessions with a vague intention of contacting the boy's family. He was convinced of this, though never made the effort. He agonized over it. He owed a debt. But what more could he have done? He knew there was no danger in the objects themselves. No one could connect them. No one would ever suspect. Even if he told someone, he couldn't prove it, and who would believe? He gathered them up and filed them away.

* * *

Within ten years, they had legalized their status, and moved into a house in Federal Heights, a suburb north of Denver. He spoke to his boys in Spanish and they responded in English. As a family, they acquired habits he considered entirely American. He obsessed over landscaping and the appearance of the house; tallied the resale value. Friday night pizza. Rockies games. The boys played baseball and he took up golf. His wife fretted over sunscreen and insect repellent. The dog slept in the house. They went to Disneyland and Las Vegas, and camped three times a year. They photographed and recorded. They collected souvenirs.

On a Saturday, a few days after the Fourth of July, Manolo's wife insisted they attend the Cherry Creek Arts Festival, and despite his reluctance, they went. The crowd was enormous. All along the streets, artists had set up canopy tents, displaying paintings or sculptures, jewelry or glass, woodwork or pottery. Heads before them bobbed, and beyond, rippled, flowed in and out of booths, here and there stopping to admire the art. Men and women wearing sandals and shorts, drinking beer and pushing strollers, following dogs on leashes. Many of them dressed worse than he would at a jobsite. Men in tank tops with thickly tattooed arms and holey jeans. One woman, the sides of her head shaved, bangs slanting down her forehead and dyed pink, wore a necklace made from chicken bones. He couldn't understand these people. They were almost entirely white, Manolo noted, holding his wife close, taking care to keep his sons near at hand. If they wandered or got too loud, he reined them in with a single look.

Late in the afternoon, when the boys were getting restless, the popsicles they ate now forgotten, clamoring for hot dogs and turkey legs and shaved ice, they came upon a booth where a man's body lie on a table, naked and perfectly still. Before the body, there was a sign that read: "The Last Illegal." A crowd had gathered round, and strangely, most were Mexican. A longhaired bearded man stalked back and forth behind the body, ignoring the gathering crowd. He looked unstable, deranged. He wore a butcher's apron splattered with blood, a shirt underneath displaying the Sacred Heart, and a Mexican presidential sash. A puckering scab ran across his forehead, and his skin was pale with makeup.

The body, Manolo learned from a Mexican nearby, was made of Jell-O. The artist had spoken at their church and invited them to take part in his performance—what he called a Perfor-MAN-cena, a ritual that would purify their souls, deepen their faith, and affirm the sacred covenant that bound them as human beings. The artist seemed to hold some power over the churchgoers, though no one could say what he intended. Manolo could tell by the submissive way they carried themselves, by the trust they granted this man, this *artist*, that they had recently arrived, had yet to be deceived. Had yet to fully compromise. Manolo would later piece together, the artist, with a sort of sick arrogance, had recruited them to serve as props to his performance.

After a while, the artist took up a butcher's knife and sharpened it on a rod, striding back and forth, only to stop and take up another, and whisk it across the rod, pausing now and again to scrape a machete over a whetstone, finally setting down the blades at the splayed feet of the body. The crowd grew, and the artist took note, stood glaring out at the crowd, and the advancing afternoon shadows. All at once he began: "Cada-ver, cada-come. That is, we see, we take in, we consume." He spoke in the voice of a carnival barker, with a hypnotizing certainty, alternating between English and Spanish.

"As a boy," he went on, "the ritual of communion disturbed me. When the priest said, 'Take, the body of Christ; Drink, the blood,' I didn't think of purification or eternal life, but

looked around guiltily and imagined Christ's flesh and blood."
Manolo felt the artist's eyes trained on him. "Pero ¿sabes qué?
Though I dreaded the guilt, I ate as others ate, because I was
hungry. Because I yearned to be part of the body.

"And we hunger. ¿Tenemos hambre, no? We are mouths.
We are need. Eating is an act of necessity, of desire and aggres-
sion. We eat to absorb, that the world might become us.
When we eat together, it is difficult to say who is eating whom.

"Like so many," he gestured to the body, "this man was
purchased at the market of Libre Comerse. A piece of mer-
chandise bought for pleasure. He was a prime specimen, every
nerve, muscle, and drop of blood, tuned to its purpose. He
suffered the torments of slow starvation, consumed piecemeal,
first his will then his spirit, till freely, he offered up his flesh
to be sold."

He gestured agonizingly, cowered, held his hands out
to placate some imagined power glowering from the tent's
roof. Expressions of anger, confusion, wonder, triumph
played across his face. He composed himself and continued:
"Through such sacrifice, El Tratado de Libre Comerse has
extended its frontier and grown its empire in the name of
progress and financial stability.

"But we cannot forget our purpose, we must honor the covenant. Art is a communal experience. A spiritual awakening,
a communion with the world. This is art." He touched the
blade to a toe of the body's splayed foot. He stood upright and
brandished the knives overhead, one in each hand poised to
strike down on the body, his face racked with maniacal rage,
and in a moment, having vanquished the spirit, he pointed
a knife at the crowd and brought their attention back to the
body.

"This body," he hovered a blade over it, "is a work of art
created to be consumed. Consumed not only through the
eyes—cada-*ver*, but,—" he made a sizzling sound with his
tongue "—savored. This work of art will circulate within us,
will course through us. We will literally digest its meaning."

He held his hands up as if to give a benediction. "Gather
round. Ven todos, ven. Come and receive the good word."
He brought his hands down and clasped them.

"Take, eat of this body.
Drink, all of you, this blood.
This debt of blood
that by its spilling,
we may be blessed,
for what trickles down,
might wash away our sins."

He bowed his head, then plunged a fist just above the body's resting hands and interlaced fingers into its chest and pulled out the heart—a green apple. "Lift up your hearts," he cried, and held up the apple for all to see, and brought it to his mouth and took a bite. He said: "Come and receive salvation."

A murmur ran through the crowd but nobody stirred. Then slowly, the applause came.

"Oye," the artist said, "a comer. Ven, ven. Yes, come, form a line." He indicated where with a point of a knife.

Manolo had rested a hand on his youngest son's shoulder, and the boy tugged at it now with both hands, rubbing his swollen hand against the boy's face, face paint smearing off on his hand. He looked at his son, face painted as Spiderman, who urged, "Come on, papa. Vamos, papa, a comer," and resisted. There was something perverse about the performance, something nauseating, not that he had understood all of what the artist had said, what point he was trying to make. The absurdity of the whole scene, the butcher-priest slash politician, the naked body, the Mexicans now lining up, the artwork they could look at but not afford, and the nonchalance of the Americans, as if this were an everyday event, unsettled him. The whole thing made him sick. His wife took his arm and he relented. They lined up behind the churchgoers.

Children nudged their way up to the table, and the adults tilted their heads, seeking a better view. He could hear the artist's voice, "Escoja su parte favorita: norte, sur, este u oeste." Sunlight glistened a dull sheen over the body's caramel skin. Strawberries outlined the body as a garnish. Its limp penis slouched between its legs like a bandaged thumb. Below the table, a sheet hung with a hundred dollar bill printed on it and above a banner read: "El Tratado de Libre Comerse: América Ge-Latina."

The artist's knife probed and sliced. Manolo could see the knife pierce the skin, and expected to see blood, but there was none. The artist pieced out the calf like slices of tube sausage, and served it on foam plates, dousing it with a blood-colored syrup and whipped cream. Those in line laughed and cringed, nervous at first, seeming to show some respect for the body. They joked about castration, but shied away. The artist commented that when men see the body of a woman they want to lick it, taste it, swallow it whole, but with a man, "Hay un tipo de nausea frente al cuerpo masculino." It's as if they can see themselves sliced, forked and eaten.

When their turn came, the boys eagerly picked out the largest pieces, sliced from the thighs, his wife a filet from the kneecap, while Manolo stood back considering the body with a hand over his mouth.

When he looked up, the artist caught his glance and gesturing at Manolo's hand, asked him, "Is that blood?"

Manolo looked at his hand, at the face paint smeared on it.

"¿Tiene las manos sucias?" the artist said and smiled.

Manolo shook his head silently, and looked down with disgust at the body.

"No se preocupe, señor, todo lo que comemos es, a la larga, carne humana." He wagged the knife at Manolo and said, "¿Sabes que? Tengo una pieza solo para usted." He stuck the knife into the body's wrist and carved around the hands and the interlaced fingers, and served it up on a plate. When he offered whip cream, Manolo shook his head, and took the plate. His wife leaned over the plate, and told him the hands seemed to be praying.

The crowd's reserve soon gave way. A boy wanted the nose, another the eyes, the ears. An American man carried the flaccid penis on his plate, impaled by a fork. After the body had been gashed, carved, scalloped, and dismembered, it felt more like a child's birthday party than a funeral banquet.

His sons held the plates close to their faces, opened their mouths wide, and with a hiss, mimicked a vampire going in for a bite. His wife nibbled away. They licked their fingers and commented that it tasted better than it looked. Manolo poked at his serving with a fork, and it trembled. He told his wife he wasn't hungry and she took his plate and wrapped it with a napkin, telling him they would take it home, put it in the freezer, and preserve it, as a souvenir.

The Lindbergh Baby

Andrés Carlstein

Ron listens to the road noise as he drives. There's the churning of the Buick's V6, the zipper-pull sound of the tires, the wind moaning on the glass. Last week he found the radio missing. Somebody must've snuck in with a coat hanger. Just another danger of parking an old car in the Bronx. Ron feels lucky to still have the car at all—he once put a bullet in the engine block when he saw someone trying to break in. That was when he first came back from the Gulf.

Jesse slumps against the door, his head sagging into the triangle of his bent arm. Is he really asleep? Ron still can't judge the meaning of the boy's behaviors. He's seen his son only a couple of times since he was a toddler. Ron learned some details about Jesse's life at the child support hearings and such, but after a while the boy himself, as a physical reality, just stopped feeling like something he needed to think about.

Yesterday they stood over Jesse's mother's grave. Car accident. The air was thick with the musk of upstate New York—fallen leaves, clean water, moist peat. She was buried in that spongy, rich earth. Ron had gotten the next-of-kin phone call and come to pick up his son. The next day there was the hollow in the ground and her casket at the bottom. Jesse stared down, mostly, and cried. When the minister finally shut up, Ron noticed Jesse glancing at him. Jesse wasn't crying right then and maybe that's why he looked, Ron thought, to see if his father was. Or maybe to show his father that he wasn't.

Jesse finally sits up and stares out the window.

"Hungry?" Ron says.

"No." Jesse runs his finger on the window, tracing some invisible thing.

"Grandma will have food. She's a good cook."

At a Shell on 17C Jesse goes into the bathroom while Ron buys half a cup of coffee and then heads outside to top it off with whiskey from a bottle in the Buick's trunk. He sets his drink in the cup holder and walks back inside. Jesse stands near the register holding a bag of candy.

"Get whatever you want," Ron says. "Just don't eat it until after dinner." As soon as he speaks he almost has to laugh. Was that him parenting?

"I've got my own money," Jesse says.

Ron was shot at once in Zakho, just after the first Gulf War. He was part of the 24th Marine Expeditionary Unit that arrived with the Guadalcanal. The 24th was the one unit in the Fleet that hadn't been rotated to the front, so they were sent to protect the Kurds in Northern Iraq. The actual war had lasted only a few days, but before things started expectations were mixed. The Iraqi Army was believed to be hardened veterans from their eight-year war with Iran. American forces had simply rolled over them. The war had come in all hard with operations named Desert Storm and Desert Shield. The 24th had no part of that. Ron and his buddies felt embarrassed to start their careers with "Operation Provide Comfort."

"Operation Desert Nanny," Acevedo said.

"Operation Sandy Drawers," Ron said.

His squad was among the first ones down. They were in a Helicopter Assault Company. Normally they should've inserted under the cover of night with Cobras and full support. Command had decided that wasn't necessary. They landed in a soccer field at midday, with the CH-46es and the CH-53 Echoes boiling the arid dust into upside-down mushroom caps. Three weeks before, the Marines had been at war with the Iraqis, but Ron's company dropped in on them that day like it was just a training exercise. Like they'd been invited over for a pickup game. Ron was convinced there'd be some remnant gunning for them. If the US lost a war with Russia and then a month later their helos dumped soldiers in a ballpark in Tennessee, who wouldn't take a shot at them? But the Iraqi Army had already retreated and Ron's company moved into the abandoned base uncontested. In the morning they set out to occupy the surrounding hills. Over the next week they swept the city to clear out any remaining weapons, and then settled into the Command dugout and foxholes where they controlled a section of road and their part of the pie surrounding the city. As far as anyone knew, the only people with guns were the Marines and the PUK militia. There were probably still a lot of service weapons and souvenirs kept by veterans from the Iran-Iraq war floating around, but command wasn't worried so neither was the average Marine.

Back then it wasn't like today. Our soldiers get killed every day now in Afghanistan, but during Desert Storm and its associated operations the Iraqi army just wasn't into it. The people didn't want to fight for Saddam. They all heard the stories. One squad of Marines came over a hill to discover half a battalion of enemy combatants with armor staring back at them. The Iraqis immediately threw down their weapons. Half a fucking battalion of men and tanks—from the fourth largest army in the world—surrendered to five jarheads scratching at sand fleas in a Humvee.

Six hundred miles to the south, Kuwaiti oil fields howled orange fire—a mist of the Earth's bile blocked out the sun and sheets of tar and burnt filth coated the sands. For the Marines in Zakho, all was calm. They'd been moving through town a couple days. There'd been no contact, no signs of opposition. The men were raw and nervous. Ron and his squad waited in an alley for the tail end of their patrol to catch up. He felt a movement across his cheek, almost like a breeze but more percussive, like a ripple. That's when the sound barrier crack of the bullet passed his head. When the shock wave whickered by, time seemed to slow.

The sniper was probably aiming for the Captain. As

designated radio operator, near-misses were part of the job. Ron had a whip antenna rising ten feet above his head, which was attached to twenty pounds of portable stove on his back (the radio generated so much heat that the men used to warm up their MREs on it). The antennae flopped and swirled above him, as if to say, hey, why not mortar this position? Take out communication and command in one shot! Ron was always jumpy. He has often reflected that if he had to go back and walk the length of that route again, there wouldn't be an apartment window he couldn't remember, a tenement doorway he couldn't recognize. He never did see the sniper. But the memory stays with him. It's not every day you kill a child.

Jesse still stares out the window as they turn up the road to Gram's house. Jesse's mother told Ron that his absence had harmed Jesse. "Broke him," was the phrase she used, more than once.

"I never see the boy," Ron told her. "You can't break what you can't see." Ron spent a lot of time not thinking about that. He's begun to think about it much more these past two days, but now she's dead so he can't argue with her anyway.

The sun is intense today. Light comes through Jesse's hair like optical fiber—so blond it's almost translucent. His mother had hair like that. Jesse also got her skin. His hair keeps falling in his face. He's almost twelve and already he's too aware of his appearance. Ron was like that in the Marines, but not because he wanted to be. You kept your shit tight or you paid for it. Maybe that's what Jesse's experiencing, in a way. Ron doubts it is vanity—Jesse seems to take no pleasure in his reflection. Probably insecurity. God forbid he get the acne I had at puberty, Ron thinks. High school will be a nightmare.

Ron has to ring the bell three times before Gram answers.

"That was fast," she says.

"Not much traffic."

"You were speeding."

"No, Gram."

"Don't lie to me." Gram presses a quivering palm to Ron's cheek. The meat of her hand is cool and yielding, like risen dough off a countertop. "You smell like hooch."

"Jesse, this is your grandmother." Ron steps aside to reveal the boy coming up behind him. She isn't his grandmother. She's his great-grandmother, but she was like a mother to Ron, so a grandmother is what she can be to Jesse. Gram switches her scowl off like a bad TV show and beams at her only great-grandchild. Jesse scans the room and fixes his gaze on an old CRT television, a hulk in the corner on four round legs, half the size of a car, the pride of her second, late husband, Ernie. She claims she gave up men because she tired of burying them. Jesse keeps looking around—at the Yankees mug on the piano, the dog hair gathered in the corners—everywhere but at her. Gram's eyes are watery but Ron can't tell if that's now just their usual state. Jesse is the last generation of her line she'll live to see. She smiles with such loving intensity that even Ron feels a bit embarrassed for the boy.

"When was the last time you fed him? For pity's sake, let's get this young man a meal." At that Jesse seems to rise within himself and he looks up at Gram for the first time.

During dinner she sits through Jesse's silence for a while, watching him when he isn't looking, like a big cat timing a lunge. After he's eaten his first serving she speaks.

"You see the rubble of that house, in the lot next door?" Gram eyes Jesse over her spectacles. "Did your father tell you why it was torn down?"

Jesse shakes his head.

"That house was haunted," Gram says.

Jesse looks up at her with hopeful disbelief, like she'd said he just won fifty dollars.

When Gram was a teenager her family came home one day and found that the neighbors had abandoned the place. They'd left the door open and a meal on the table. Just dropped everything and went away. She tells Jesse about the knocking sounds, and how the family's youngest daughter once followed a disembodied voice up to the attic and was locked inside by some unknown force.

"Her father found her wearing only her small clothes," Gram says. "She'd hung her dress to flap out the garret window, which she'd broken open. She had no other way to get help. She was up there for only a day but she'd screamed herself hoarse and didn't talk again for weeks. We always assumed those people were just a bit off. The next family that moved in did no better. They packed up and left within three months. The house stayed vacant after that."

As teenagers Ron and his friends explored that old building, trying to scare themselves. All they ever found were empty beer cans, used rubbers, and smashed windowpanes. The place was finally bulldozed before it could collapse on somebody. Funny, Ron thinks, forgot all about that haunted house.

Gram and Jesse get up from the table to look out the window, and she puts her hand on his shoulder as she talks and points. Just like that she's got him. She snatches something beyond Ron's reach so easily that for a moment he almost resents bringing the boy here. He imagines that as a young woman Gram felled giants with a smile—just dropped men flat on their faces.

Gram puts Jesse to sleep in Ron's old room. After helping her clean up Ron goes to check on him. He must've heard me coming, Ron thinks, because Jesse is turned over with his back to him as Ron walks in. He sits down on the bed. Tiny cross-country trophies from Ron's middle school days race in static strides along a shelf—injection molded and coated in metallic plastic, they are the kind given to everyone who shows up. Ron looks at his boy and feels a pooling nausea. Maybe it's that sensation, or seeing how easily Gram got to Jesse, but he is overcome with a strange need to connect with his son. Ron sits there a long time trying to form words. He's startled when Jesse speaks first.

"What do you want?"

Ron recovers quickly. "Just came to talk."

"About what."

Ron glances around, his mind turning. Nothing comes. After a while Jesse rolls over to look at him. Ron finds himself unable to meet Jesse's gaze.

"Listen," Ron says. "About your mother . . ."

"I wish it was you," Jesse says, flat and clear. Just like that.

This seems like something that should make Ron mad but it doesn't. Oddly it makes him feel better. It's right. Ron can't think of how to say that in a way that would make sense to Jesse, because it doesn't even make sense to him, entirely.

"Why don't you just go away," Jesse says.

Ron detects no resentment in his voice. Mostly boredom. The bed makes a muted creak as Ron stands up and leaves the room.

Gram pours herself another whiskey as they sit on the deck. Clouds obscure a bright moon. The diffused glow comes through to them as ashy light. The fireflies have already faded away, the hour too late for them.

"Why'd you come here?" Gram says.

"Shouldn't a boy know his family?"

"That's some question." She doesn't say it spitefully. He feels the slap of it regardless.

"I get that."

"You better not be here doing what I think you're doing," Gram says.

Ron looks down and puts an elbow on his knee. His fingertips touch his brow and he realizes he's trying to cover his face. He puts his hand on his lap and straightens up.

"Aren't you tired of this?"

"Yes ma'am, I am tired."

"What if I die? Who'll look out for him then? You thought of that?" she says. "You're doing something I can't let happen."

"I've done lots of things you wouldn't."

She pauses at this and looks out at the distance. Maybe she's checking the topography of what Ron said, a place she's never been, to see if there's a safe way through. After a moment more she says, "We all do things."

"Not like what I did."

"Oh no? You know my whole life? You know where I've been?" She pulls another ice cube from the box on the table and puts it in her glass. "You want to go on forever feeling sorry? You aren't the only one you're punishing."

Ron swears quietly and starts to get up.

"You sit down," Gram says. She doesn't speak angrily. She's not commanding. She just talks like she's stating what she knows he has to do. She says it the way some women can, the way that takes all the fight out of the thing with just her sound.

As if sitting back down is like the sun coming up. He sits.

There wasn't much combat in Operation Provide Comfort. The only action Ron ever saw was that one time he received fire and shot back. He was twenty. They'd been trained to shoot well. In boot camp he achieved the highest qualification on the range: Expert Marksman. Under ideal conditions he could easily shoot a tight grouping in the chest of a man-sized target at 500 meters with just standard rounds and iron sights. Many Marines could. He didn't fault his training for his actions. And he couldn't blame instinct or nerves. Nor could he say youthful zeal was the cause. All the Marines were young and skittish and well trained. Perhaps the awareness of his mortality, scrawled daily through the sky by a floppy antenna, played a role. Whatever it was, the near-miss of that gunshot certainly rattled him, as such events can. But he didn't feel particularly inclined to give himself excuses for his lack of discipline. They'd all been trained to take life. They all secretly wondered what that training amounted to. You don't raise baby tigers and expect them to grow up to be sheep.

Of his group, he was the only one who returned fire. Everyone else froze or followed protocol and took cover to wait for orders. Everyone else reacted more or less the same to the first bullet sent their way. Everyone but him.

The bullet came from behind. After the boom went off in his ear as the shock wave passed, he immediately turned and sighted a silhouette in a window and fired. He just spun around and shot. What a shot. A trick marksman at a rodeo show couldn't do what he did five times out of ten. His weapon had been pointed down for safety. He pulled the rifle to bear in one fluid motion, aligned the sights across the target in the window, and squeezed the trigger in passing. It's closer to say he slung that bullet.

He'd turned in the presumed direction of fire and his eye had locked onto a silhouette in a window. It wasn't the sniper. Turned out to be a boy who'd been watching the American soldiers as they moved through his town. The bullet hit the kid in the face and went out the back of his head. The insides of his skull painted the wall behind him in an oval swatch of pink and red, like Ron later saw Jesse do to the floor with his Spaghetti-O's when he was two. Ron was the last in his squad to hit the stairs. They'd run inside to clear the building and just as Ron got there he felt them pushing him back, trying to stop him from seeing what he'd done. He could still see it over their helmets, the pieces sliding down the wall, the dark blood pouring over the dusty landing. The bright red blood you get from a cut on your finger is nothing. It's when you see that deep black blood that you need to worry about someone's life. That's the mortal blood. His squad leader held him by the webbing of his gear and pulled him out of the entryway. Acevedo, the squad's gunner and Ron's best friend, slammed on his chest and screamed over and over to back the fuck up. They were trying to protect him from what he'd done. They never found the real shooter. Ron thought later about how he'd just taken a kid's life for nothing, and his friends thought it would make a difference if he didn't see it.

He wasn't court-martialed, but he was disciplined. The newspapers reported on it. He was told that wasn't the kind of press they needed for the war effort. That wasn't the "comfort" they were supposed to provide. He was sent to psych. They said he could get counseling through the VA after he got out, but he never much liked sharing his business with people he didn't know. The Captain in psych already knew the story anyway so he talked because they said it would help. Ron guessed that it did help, maybe. Didn't really matter, though. What matters is that he still sees the boy's pieces on the wall. The dark blood on the dirty staircase.

Gram leans back in her chair. They are silent a long time. If he could tell anyone ever, it'd be her, right then. Something wells up in him but he can't quite say it. Instead he closes his eyes and swallows his whiskey, getting the burnt peat with hints of hickory and leather. He tries to think about the taste, to focus on anything other than what comes to his head by default. Ron swirls the drink in his hand, tries to savor it. Gram keeps much better spirits than he can afford. The sound of the ice against his glass is barely audible. What a riot crickets and bullfrogs make in a field at night.

Gram starts to talk. After a time Gram speaks of how the family came to Odessa. He knows part of this story. They moved here to start a chicken farm. The area is still mainly agricultural. Gram's father was an engineer and they'd lived in Hoboken, New Jersey, where Gram was born. It was the Great Depression and, like most everyone else, her father had lost his job. A common story.

"Papa arranged the chairs and mattresses and steamer trunks on a flatbed," she says. "He tied it all down with precision. A beautiful web, now that I think on it. Uncle Danny drove the truck. Papa took all of us along behind in the Nash. That was a great car. We were fortunate. We were on a waiting list for eight months to get it. Nash couldn't build them fast enough. My sister Nancy was just a toddler, you know, and she was asleep on the bench seat next to me in the back. I'll never forget it. March 2, 1932." Gram reaches up to wipe at something on her cheek—an invisible insect, or a memory of one. "We were on the road so early, coming through New Jersey. There was a roadblock along the way. That was the morning after the Lindbergh boy went missing. It was a national outrage. I was just a child and couldn't understand it. Seemed to me the whole adult world was breaking apart. There were flashing lights and hollering and car horns, even so early in the morning. People were afraid. At the checkpoint they stood Papa and Uncle Danny on one side of the road. I remember the policemen with their slickers and shotguns. They made Mama wake Nancy up and undress her. Nancy had to stand naked in front of Mama and Papa and Uncle Danny and all those strangers. They had to prove she wasn't a boy child. The cops needed to be sure before they let us go. Mama stripped Nancy and she wobbled there in the cold, wailing and holding Mama's hands, the rain splatters on her naked legs and leather booties.

"In the car I asked Mama why they made us show Nancy with her clothes off. Mama didn't look back as she said, 'Because some idiot doesn't know how to lock his damn door.'"

Half an hour goes by and the sounds of the outside night still. They are quiet all this time, Gram and Ron. They listen together to the quiet. She clears her throat with a wet growl and stands up.

"I'm not going to tell you what to do," she says. "You're grown."

She walks by him and puts a soft hand on his shoulder as she passes. He feels a heavier pressure, as if she almost falls. The move to simply comfort becomes one to keep her feet. Ron starts to shake involuntarily. She stops dead, her hand still. They hang there the two of them, quivering, as if suspended by strings. Finally she puts her other hand on his head. He begins to weep, his hands in his lap and his ear on her belly, smelling baby powder and the piece of trout she dropped on herself during dinner.

Ron is alone for a long time after Gram goes to bed. He remembers calling home from the phone booth on the base after the war, listening through the crackling line, as intently as he'd ever done. He strained to hear the gurgles and hums of his newborn, as if the boy had something important to tell him. As if his child could utter a sound that might transform him. Soldiers today have computers and can see the faces of their families back home. Ron would've sprinted through a minefield to see what Jesse looked like. His mother told Ron what she'd named him and Ron said it again and again in his mind. Like an ancient prayer-sound he repeated the word daily and it carried him through the tour, through his interminable service, through all that time when he still believed he might come back home like Zakho had never happened.

As he sits in Gram's house the urge to escape, to race back to the Bronx, almost overtakes him. Panic builds in his chest, nearly forcing him out to the car. Instead he sits. He waits it out, listening. He imagines Gram telling him to sit. The only way I can leave, he decides, is if I can be back home and passed out drunk before Jesse wakes. He knows that he must be unconscious before Jesse comes to in this unfamiliar room and recognizes, in that place that feels the truth before it can be spoken, that his father is gone and not coming back.

When Ron was a Marine he called his fellow Marines brothers. He would have given his life to save any one of them. All that for people he no longer even speaks to. Strangers. Ron stands, decided. He walks as quietly as he can to his old room. He pushes the door. Ron's eyes open to the dark until he sees shapes and the separation of dark from lighter dark. He can just make out Jesse laying facedown on the bed—his blond hair reflecting the window's soft glow. The shadows in the room settle where the light cannot reach, with valleys and blackness in the deepest parts. The trophies shine dull gold and Ron thinks, my child is here in this room. That is my living son. He moves forward and slowly kneels beside the bed. Reaching out, he holds his hand above Jesse's back, between the small shoulder blades. There is just the air of him beneath Ron's hand, the heat of him, until the pads of his fingers meet the cotton of Jesse's shirt. The boy is so still and warm under his palm. Ron feels the tension in Jesse's back and realizes he must be awake. Maybe he was never asleep.

Suddenly Jesse turns over and grips Ron's wrist with both hands, pulling Ron's arm to his chest. Jesse's face is clenched as he hangs on. He has never looked more childlike. Jesse embraces Ron's hand as if it were his whole body—as if he's afraid to ask more of his father than just a single limb.

Ron stays there still and quiet, afraid to move. After a moment, without thinking about it, he stands up, one hand still holding onto Jesse's, and takes off his shoes and socks. He lies down on the bed. The creaks eventually stop as he settles onto his back. Ron closes his eyes and listens to Jesse breathing. Over time the breaths even out.

Bright sunlight is everywhere in the room. Ron doesn't understand where he is, at first. When he remembers he turns his head and Jesse is gone. Ron is alone in the bed. There's a rising panic in him and he sits up with it. From the kitchen he hears silverware clanking on a plate, then Gram's voice. There's eggs and toast. And coffee. She's made breakfast. He hears Jesse's soft reply to Gram. He's surprised at his feeling of relief.

Ron stands; his bare feet press flat on the cool, wood floor. His hands go up to his head to smooth his hair. He's still a bit drunk and almost has to sit back down on the bed. Instead, he keeps his feet and takes an uneasy step toward the kitchen, holding one arm out for balance.

Hippos

Laurie Baker

We were thinking about seeing the hippos. At Lake St. Lucia, you could hire a motorboat for practically nothing. It was highlighted in most of the guides.

This was around Easter. It was getting cold, but the weather was good. We were on ten days vacation. We'd traveled to Durban, then north up the coast. We'd come to St. Lucia for the wetlands. We arrived in the middle of the day and found accommodation at the St. Lucia Wilds, which had self-catering apartments. These were freestanding and in the shape of rondavels. They were clean and dimly lit. They had thatched roofs. I inspected the rooms. There was one with twin beds for Ephraim and Jonas, and a loft for me. The bathroom was spotless. A sticker on the mirror pictured hippos frolicking in the water; it said: "Water is precious, don't waste it." Later I would try to peel this sticker off to take with me, but it wouldn't come off so easily. I would scratch it until it was wrecked.

After we unpacked, we walked down the main street for lunch. It went through the town's center, which was nothing much. The sky was so pale it was practically white.

Soon I was standing at the counter of a take-away called The Hippo Butchery, where Jonas had ordered three half loaves filled with stew. One for him, one for Ephraim, and one for me, although I hadn't asked for it and didn't want it. Ephraim and Jonas had left me to wait for the food, and found seats across the room. They sat at a square wooden table with short legs. They hunched over it like men playing chess.

Earlier that day, I'd told them I'd changed my mind. We were an hour south of St. Lucia and I'd been watching the scenery, which looked beautiful but worn, like a vanquished kingdom. For a long time I'd felt like crying. Then I told them I didn't want to see the hippos, even though seeing them had been my idea in the first place. Jonas laughed, thinking I was making a joke; Ephraim, driving, said nothing. No joke, I said; there were dangers I just hadn't considered before. And although this was mostly untrue—I'd known the risks all along—I'd been surprised by a feeling, over the last few days, of exposure and defenselessness, as if the odds of my being picked out by an arbitrary moment of misfortune had increased a hundred fold. But this was not an explanation I could give. What did they want from me? Not indecision certainly, not paranoia or doubt. And not love, it seemed, either—it was Ephraim whom I had slept with, once, months before, Ephraim for whom my longing was like a tattered flag, resolutely held aloft, Ephraim who'd said, with bewildered irritability, "Do you think it is possible? I'm not thinking it's possible." Whether he meant a relationship between a white, American woman and an African, or between him and me, I wasn't sure.

I waited for the stews, which were called Bunny Chow. It was an African dish. You scooped out the insides of half a loaf of bread and used the crust as a bowl.

Ephraim and Jonas didn't put much stock in my counsel; they wanted to see the hippos anyway. They said there was too little chance they'd ever be "this side" again. That's how they put it, Africans did—this side, that side—indicating any place different from where they were or where they'd come from. About America, they asked me, "How is it, that side?" and I'd feel the vastness of time and space and think how remarkable that a person could conquer it, a person like me. And they were right; there *was* little chance, although I didn't think they were trying to manipulate me. They meant, only, that tourism was a luxury for them, a gift they weren't likely to waste money on, if ever they had money to waste.

The trip itself was my idea, the cost covered entirely by money I'd earned or been given. Jonas and Ephraim had grown up in the homelands: villages without an infrastructure, shrinking houses in squares of dirt. This was in the seventies, with apartheid still at the top of its game. They had had the basics back then, sometimes less; now a teacher's salary and money to send home. I got a small stipend from the Church, a hundred bucks a month, which I spent on batteries for my Walkman and overseas postage and snacks. I was beginning, after so many months, to think of the time I lived here less as the noble, idealistic gesture everyone seemed to think it (even the Africans, who assumed, incorrectly, that I was stoically homesick) than as a peculiarly incautious break from the real design of my life. I worried that I wouldn't understand, in the long run, why I'd given my time so eagerly away.

But I had savings and a credit card, not money to burn but enough to be generous. I wanted to be generous. Ephraim had been twice to Johannesburg but no farther, Jonas not once even south of Lebowa. I was eager to show them the world they belonged to but had never seen.

So the itinerary was set up by me. My authority on the matter was simultaneously undesirable and inadequate. A week ago, I would have done anything to please them.

It was our ninth day of vacation. In less than twenty-four hours, we'd be heading back to school, classes to resume the day after. I imagined my students finding out how I'd spent my vacation, teasing me for having traveled with two unmarried men. My students badgered me with questions about my views on love: Would I ever date an African? Would I marry him and live here forever? However, they never did the same with Ephraim and Jonas, their African teachers, who were so fierce and unyielding in their discipline, their sense of decorum and respect. With me, the students were relaxed, boisterous, affectionate. Sometimes I felt I was like a child to them.

And what would I tell them? The trip had been a disappointment.

We'd woken early and headed north to St. Lucia on the N-2. The drive took us past historic strongholds of Zulu warriors, coastal towns once razed by racial conflict, now spots for battlefield walks and workshops about Zulu medicine and music. Neither Ephraim nor Jonas was Zulu; they talked about the blood-thirst of past warriors and tsk-tsked in rebuke. I knew about the Zulu nation, saw something proudly masculine in their poison-dipped spears, their dark, gleaming chests. By comparison, Jonas and Ephraim were like partners in comedy, the classic image of fat and thin. Jonas was always laughing and smiling. He was from Venda. You could tell if you knew what to look for. He had the tribal scars: a pair of half-inch knife cuts on each cheek. He had a soft, boyish, gentle look.

Ephraim was Northern Sotho, very dark and good-looking and serious about how he presented himself. He headed up a local faction of the African National Congress. He was authoritative and disciplined but frail-looking, too, in his neatly pressed trousers and collared shirts. He had a skin condition that made his body look splotched with dust.

We drove in silence, or listened to ABBA, or gossiped about students. Sometimes Ephraim and Jonas talked in Sotho, and I paid attention to the intonations of their speech, trying to figure out if the topic was serious or carefree.

St. Lucia was small-scale but warranted preservation. The guide gave it a complimentary write-up. The lake had freshwater sharks and crocodiles, but these were not the animals you were likely to see. The hippos were ubiquitous, if you rented a boat and took it to the interior. The hippos were the reason to come. I'd heard the warnings, of course—hippos cause more human deaths than any other animal on the *continent*—but the perils of the African wilderness struck me as too arbitrary to worry about.

But suddenly, mere hours from the place, I found myself arguing that the setup itself was haphazard and ill-conceived. I was gleaning this from the guide. "Look," I said, and read aloud: "*There are boats for hire on just about any spot you can enter the water. These one-man businesses are highly competitive; be prepared for several to fight for the sale.* See? No safeguards, no liability." I waved the book around.

Jonas clapped his hand to his mouth in a way that made him look dumbfounded.

"I'm not believing that," he said. "Are they letting us do a fool's errand? No, I don't think so."

And who was this *they*? I wanted to ask.

All over Africa were attractions like this, ecotourism without an infrastructure, self-guided and unsupervised. Ephraim and Jonas didn't see the problem. I could come up with any number of reasons it was a bad idea *just* by keeping in mind severe personal injury.

I gave them the facts. Hippos are *killers*. They're fast, aggressive, and mean. Their great talent is that they don't look it. They project apathy and a lack of intelligence. They instill complacency by reminding you of farm animals: docile and unassuming, wild but almost cuddly.

But here was the kicker, I said. Unlike lions, who may or may not want to eat you, hippos are *herbivores*. Vegetarians! Their attacks are *personal*. Their look says, *Get out of my goddamned way*. It says: *Your ass is mine*.

Ephraim and Jonas laughed. Jonas turned around in his seat up front—Ephraim was driving and I was in back—and said good-naturedly, "Aie, wena! You are just exaggerating! You are not really thinking these things."

I stretched out on the back seat and put my bare feet against the window glass. "I'm not exaggerating." I pressed my feet against the glass and wondered how much pressure before it cracked. The hippos were beside the issue, I wanted to say. What did it matter whether we saw the hippos as long as we were together? And how come I *always* got stuck in back? The car had been rented in *my* name.

I sat up abruptly and met Ephraim's eyes in the rearview mirror.

"Decide when we get there?" he said. His compromise shamed me. I caught sight of my face and thought about how my mother used to call me Gertrude or Prudence whenever I was in a bad mood. She'd do it to get me to laugh; I'd stare her down, unflinching.

The first time I saw Ephraim and Jonas was shortly after

my arrival. School was about to start. I'd come several days earlier, but the African teachers started trickling in the day before classes. We all lived in the teachers' compound. I had my own flat, a couple of rooms, the last in a row on the woman's side. For an hour or two that afternoon, I sat on the stoop in the open doorway, feeling the summer heat as if it could strike me blind. Now and then a teacher came by to greet me. Ephraim and Jonas were playing cards across the compound. They were straddling a bench. They were sharing a liter of Coke, using both hands to swig from it. The compound was a swath of dirt, no plants, little grass, a single tree they'd moved the bench beneath for shade. The tree had little yellow blossoms, some of which had fallen to the ground. The whole scene had a photogenic dreaminess to it. I wanted to get my camera. But taking a picture of them would have made me a tourist, and a tourist was exactly what I didn't want to be.

The stews were taking a long time.

Customers came and went, ordering T-bones with pap or taking their supper home raw, in white butcher's paper. All were African, some openly curious about me, others indifferent or oblivious. A man came to the counter and leaned into me, his shoulder pressing against mine, his hard fingers against my leg. He turned to look at me.

I looked back. The moment was like a showdown, until he laughed and turned away. I realized I was sweating. I was unhappy to think I could be frightened by such a man, but unhappier, still, to think that his attention was something I was slow to reject.

I wasn't scared living here. And I was proud of my fearlessness, as if it proved something impressive or dependable about my character. There was plenty to worry about—car-jackings, ritual killings, malaria—but none of it was likely to touch me; even the political instability felt like a thrilling, off-stage event, something to take the edge off of a monotonous day.

The man had gone. For the moment, there were no other customers. I put my elbows up on the counter. Someone had left a copy of *The Star*. The front page led with news we'd heard earlier that day on the radio. It was a big story, the kind that got the hasty, voracious attention of the world. The man responsible for planning the politically motivated death of Chris Hani, assassinated a couple of weeks earlier, had been arrested. The man was a member of the Conservative party. A Polish immigrant had pulled the trigger, killing Hani in front of his home in a racially mixed suburb of Boksburg, but this man, an Afrikaner, had put in the order.

There was a picture of him. He was thin, dressed in a coat and tie, with oversized square glasses. He looked as harmless as an elementary school teacher, with his tweed suit and limp, graying hair.

Chris Hani had headed up the Communist Party and the armed wing of the African National Congress. He'd been hugely popular. After his murder, Mandela had addressed the nation, a stoic voice appealing for right-mindedness. What he'd said had made me want to take up arms: "A white man, full of prejudice and hate, came to our country and committed a deed so foul that our whole nation now teeters on the brink of disaster."

But Mandela wasn't calling for retribution or violence. He wanted a harmonious solution, a racial compromise. Was there something to what *I* was doing, then? A white woman traveling with African men; was this something, in its own way, that had initiative and value?

Hani had been killed a few days before vacation. There were rallies all over the place, a mood of keyed-up bitterness. Even the students held a demonstration on the school stage, which the white missionaries in charge indulged out of a respect for political enlightenment. By the time vacation had started, emotions were used up, and everyone went home cheerfully. Ephraim, Jonas, and I hitchhiked into town to pick up the car. I'd found a deal at a cheap garage called Piet's. Its namesake was an anemic white guy, tattoo-sleeved, with long, thinning hair. He'd advertised the car in the paper; he didn't want to get rid of it but he didn't have much use for it either. He came out into the junkyard where we were waiting and snapped a rag at a rheumy-eyed dog barking at us.

I followed him to his office. We went through the rental

agreement. The form had been written out in pen on lined paper, hardly a binding document.

Ephraim and Jonas waited outside in the junkyard, talking with the black men who worked there. They sat on inverted buckets. I waited for Piet to ask me how we knew each other, or why we were together.

I jotted down information. On most forms my personal data was unremarkable. Caucasian female, 18-25. Here I checked a box that said FOREIGNER and then Piet asked what kind.

"American," I said and Piet wrote this under FOREIGNER, adding a line of exclamation points. The points were intended to look hostile, I guessed, but gave an impression of childishness instead.

Piet put the pen down. He looked hard at me, and I knew what was coming. "Don't fucking play with fire, man." He took my check and stared at it. He flicked at the corner where my name and address were written. "Does your father know where you are?" he said. "Give me his number and I'll call him. I'll tell him where you are."

I was used to such outbursts. I'd always dismissed them as racial paranoia; now, I felt half-glad for the concern.

Halfway through our trip, Ephraim would forget to check the fuel indicator and we would run out of gas on the highway. I would find myself furious with his carelessness; I would sulk in the back of the car. He and Jonas would walk to a petrol station. You stay behind, they said. Someone to protect the car, they said. See you soon, they said, but they'd be gone for hours. I would read a book during that time; I would cry; pee in the grass. I would think about how Ephraim had refused to find a place for me in his concept of life's best virtues, not, as I was so firmly determined to believe, because he didn't love me back, but because for him I would always be a moving target, an impossible spot to lay his head.

"Of course he knows," I said. "My father knows everything."

Piet shrugged. He gave me a key tied to a bit of string.

The African preparing our stews was staring at me. I smiled; he looked away. A minute or two later, he rushed over and spread the newspaper on the counter out in front of me, pointing at the grainy photograph of a white girl, a blonde, standing on a large rock with her arms flung wide. She looked wildly happy.

He said, "I thought I am seeing a ghost!" and leaned forward across the counter, trying to read the paper upside down. He had watery eyes and teeth as white as paint.

I skimmed the article he was talking about. The girl had been killed by a hippo the morning before while boating in the Lake St. Lucia estuary. The girl was an American. She'd been a teacher living in Zululand. She'd been in Africa for over a year. She was 5'7", 130 pounds. She was twenty-three but looked younger. In all ways, except for the color of our hair, we were the same.

The words on the page were small and black; the ink on my fingers left half-moon prints on the paper's edge.

A local doctor had been interviewed. He'd inspected the body, which he'd described as "expertly mauled."

"I thought it was you," said the man happily. "You!"

He put his hand over his heart.

"It was beating," he said. "I told myself, no. Then I wondered, even, if she's your sister, your twin."

I shook my head. I studied the picture. We didn't actually look at all alike, but I felt oddly possessive of the story, as if I had personally known the girl.

A white woman came up beside me. She wasn't looking at either of us; she was looking at everything on the shelves beneath the counter and in the glass case and talking straightaway about what she wanted. She had a bland, efficient voice. She wanted a loaf of bread, a piece of meat, coleslaw. She had big hair, dyed blond. The man was quiet while he got what she wanted. The coleslaw was red, made from beets. She noticed me then and looked slightly astonished. She took her things and left.

The man told me that his name was Archybold. He said, "Are you with them?"

"Them?" I pointed to Jonas and Ephraim.

He nodded.

"Yes."

"You like blacks, then," he said.

"Why shouldn't I?" I said.

He thought about that. "Are you married?"

"I'm too young for that."

"Are you a Boer, then?"

"That's crazy," I said. "Of course I'm not a Boer."

Archybold thought this was very funny. He cleaned the sweat from his face with the skin of his arm and said, "You must give me your address, we must be pen pals." Then he pushed a crumpled bit of napkin across the counter.

"Sure," I said, while he found a pen.

I pressed down too hard with the pen and tore the napkin. He shouted something over to Jonas and Ephraim, and Ephraim said, "US of A," and Archybold whistled. He watched me write. It was like signing an autograph.

The stews were ready to eat. Archybold ceremoniously set them on the counter, and I gave him the napkin.

"These stews come with pap," he told me.

"Great," I said. "I love pap."

"You love pap!" He shook his head. "You're not a Boer, like you said."

"Have you noticed that Boers are very big people?" I said. I indicated the spot where the white woman had just stood. "Plus they have an accent. They're like Germans."

"Like Germans," Archybold repeated.

"Watch out," I said. "Apartheid might be dead, but these Boers are waiting for a resurrection."

This was something I'd heard Ephraim say. Ephraim hated the Afrikaners. That was why he taught Afrikaans. The fact that it was no longer required in high school curriculums meant nothing to him; it was a trick by Boers, he told me, "and if you are wet behind the ears, you'll fall down dead."

Archybold nodded soberly. He suddenly remembered the stews. "Go," he said. "Sit. I'm bringing these now-now." He carried the three stews at once.

He greeted Jonas and Ephraim and they greeted him back. He shook their hands and shook mine.

"One of these good days I'll get to the US of A," he told me, and smiling, went back to his counter.

I ate the stew, breaking off pieces of crust to sop up the

gravy.

I showed Ephraim and Jonas the article on the dead girl. There was a photo of a hippo, sitting with its huge jaws open. The caption read: "Yawning threat display." Hippos, the article said, were responsible for 400 human deaths.

"Is that 400 deaths in all time?" I said. "Or 400 a year?"

Jonas shrugged. He was eating his stew intently.

"Ever," he said.

"A year," Ephraim said.

Jonas took the newspaper and read a little and pointed at the picture of the girl. "Did you know this lady?"

"You always seem to think that all Americans must know each other," I said.

"You don't?" he said, surprised.

"America is huge. Do you know all Africans?"

"In Venda, practically."

"Venda is very small."

We talked about what it must have been like for the girl. I shivered theatrically. I told them that a hippo will butt its head against you until you are unconscious. Then you drown. I butted my own head against Jonas's shoulder and he laughed.

"You are full of facts," Ephraim said.

We finished our stews. "Let's see them," said Jonas.

I said OK. "It's even safer now," I told them, and pointed to the dead girl, then folded her back up and left her on the chair. "The odds are with us."

"The odds are with us," echoed Jonas.

We gathered up our things. Ephraim walked ahead, and I hurried to catch up.

"Lifejackets cost extra," I read aloud from the guide.

As we walked outside, we waved goodbye to Archybold— "One of these good days I will get to the US of A!" he repeated—and I put on my sunglasses.

Jonas said, "Let me have those."

I gave them to him. We crossed the street and Ephraim and Jonas went into a small, concrete building that housed the public toilets. I stood outside. The white woman from the take-away was walking on the other side of the street; she saw me and crossed, looking left and right for traffic. She halted in front of me and shifted her food bag from one shoulder to the other.

"The world has got it wrong about us," she said.

"What?"

"You try living here," she said.

I said, "I *am* living here."

She said that the worst thing about the end of apartheid were all the crowds. Blacks in the shopping malls, blacks in the cinemas, blacks at the beach. She ticked these off with her fingers. She had thick, painted fingernails.

"What are you talking about?" I said. I looked for Ephraim and Jonas.

Ephraim and Jonas came out of the toilets, and the woman went away once again. I told them what she'd said. They shook their heads and told me it was a bitter pill I was learning to swallow.

We walked toward the lake. I felt happy. I wondered if Ephraim and Jonas thought about happiness in the same way, as something sly and powerfully unpredictable, a thing incomplete and treacherous and monumental.

We rented a motorboat: a functional little thing with two oars and a bucket, just in case. These were so obvious as signs of warning that I pointed them out and laughed; the guy renting to us had thrown them in for free.

"No lifejackets?" I asked him.

He went into a shed and came out empty-handed, shaking his head.

"I guess not," I said.

He started negotiating with Jonas and Ephraim. Already the cost was next to nothing, but the three of them seemed to think that a few minutes' haggling was necessary.

Who's winning? I thought, spectating from my seat in the boat, shored in the mud.

Hippos!

We came across a small group of four, their ears poking

out of the water. I had my camera and Jonas had a disposable one and my binoculars around his neck and Ephraim was in charge of steering. Jonas couldn't believe it, he stood up in the boat and snapped a dozen pictures in a single go.

We drove on. For a long time we didn't see much. We drove lazily, our eyes aching against the sun.

I ran my fingers through the water. It was murky and opaque, a frisson of gleam on its surface with the texture and glint of coal.

"The animals are napping," Jonas said.

"*I'm* napping," I said.

Then around a bend: a pod of hippos, twenty or more.

"Jack is the pot!" shouted Jonas.

We watched them, riveted. They barely moved. Water lapped around their heads. Ephraim shaded his eyes with his hand.

"It's so familial," I said. "I wonder who bitches about who?"

There were babies in the group, babies or teenagers. It was hard to tell. "Cute," I said and actually cooed.

What happened next was neither inevitable nor random chance. It lay somewhere in the twilight between the two, in the place where memory resides, caught between what we force upon ourselves and what forces itself on us. We were hit from beneath, and the boat lifted up on one side, then plunged in again with the rolling motion of a seesaw, the spray of water in my face like a benediction. Jonas cried out. The hippo had risen out of the water, mouth wide as if to consume us.

Ephraim tried gunning the motor, once, twice. It caught, and suddenly we were gone, retreating, with water up to our ankles and the sun at our backs. The hippo had disappeared. I thought about how close it had been, so close I could have touched it. And I might have, too, had I not been knocked to my hands and knees in the cold, shallow bottom of the boat. I stayed there like that: light, helpless, a girl for whom dreams had split open and reformed themselves. And I looked up at Ephraim, a man whose life desires eclipsed my own—what was it he kept trying to tell me?

Climb On

Shubha Venugopal

Ashoke eased his truck through the park under a sky shot with cobalt. It was not yet dawn. He drove slowly, avoiding jackrabbits and kangaroo rats that flicked by like illusions. Dispersed across the flatness lay massive heaps of stones, their black silhouettes resembling rubble. The ruins of a civilization inhabited by giants.

When he stopped at the north side of Joshua Tree park, he left the headlights on. The lights cast distorted shadows onto the hard clay where he and Sara sorted their gear. Sara's shadow stretched longer than his, though she stood a foot shorter; she stepped farther from the truck and said, "My shadow's dwarfing yours."

Ashoke, checking slings, webbing, harnesses, carabineers, didn't respond: he was thinking about his dog, Pepper, and his clash with Sara. After he placed the smaller items into the appropriate piles, he moved to the ropes. He handed Sara the lighter rope—the 9.4 mm with bright blue and orange stripes, which she dropped into a messy heap.

"I can handle the other just as easy," she said about the rope he held. "You don't have to carry the heavier one."

Instead of offering her his faded 10.5 mm, he placed it near his boots.

"Fine," she said, turning her back.

He shook his head. He outweighed her by eighty-five

pounds.

She'd been bugging him to get a new rope, so he got her a new one, though he still brought along his favorite. It felt strange listening to her advice; he'd grown accustomed to being her teacher, even after they became lovers.

With graceful, measured movements, he swung a bite of rope from one side of his neck to another in butterfly coils until it resembled a backpack. He tied the ends around his chest.

"It's the 'turtle-building-its-shell' dance," Sara said, her voice falsely cheerful. She was overcompensating because of their argument, he knew. And she was tired.

"Aren't they born with shells?"

"You could play along sometimes." She coiled her own rope and complained, "I'm so jerky compared to you."

"You're fine." He didn't tell her he thought her rope poorly wrapped.

When he finished securing his rope to his back, he reached for hers too.

"I've got it," she said, backing away.

He took it anyway, slinging it over his muscled arm. "It's no trouble. Watch your footing; it's dark."

They finished packing their gear bags and set off, the silence broken only by the hum of a distant airplane and the scuffling of rodents among the cholla. Warped cacti jutted their thorns toward them. It was earlier than most climbers arrived at the park; Ashoke hoped to claim their routes by reaching the cliff before anyone else. Despite the hint of gold tinting the eastern sky, the moon lingered above them, gilding Sara's fair hair. Today, he'd help Sara hone her skills on difficult 5.11+ routes. She hoped to do the big walls one day, such as the multi-day climbs on Yosemite's El Capitan and Half Dome. He wanted her fully prepared before rushing into routes longer and more complicated than she'd attempted.

Her idea of fully prepared wasn't his and she chafed under his protection. It didn't matter. He walked ahead on trails, scoping for obstacles that might hurt her: rattlesnakes, poisoned-tipped thorns, blade-edged rocks. He flung his arm across her chest when he braked the truck too hard, and relieved her from lifting weighty loads. When she lead-climbed tricky routes, he grew tense, edgy.

They'd met a year and a half before. She had never climbed. He'd been climbing for a decade. He was thirty-seven, she, twenty-two. He managed Boulder Run—the small outdoor gear shop not far from the park's entrance, and also taught rock climbing classes.

She'd headed straight for him when she first entered the shop, latent energy in her limbs, sexiness in her stride. He leaned over the glass display, his hands spread wide, his white-tipped fingers bent sharply over the edges. She said she wanted a job to help pay for climbing classes. Her open face, and the corners of her shapely lips curled into a smile, told him she'd be good with customers.

She became his student, taking one course after another, and proclaimed him a good teacher—quiet and patient. They rarely climbed apart. Now, she boasted she could almost out-climb him, but he didn't believe it, no matter what she said. He couldn't help it. With her short, boyish haircut and smooth, freckled skin, she could pass for a teenager—her head not even close to reaching his shoulders.

In recent weeks, Sara had been restless, yearning for new mountain ranges. Fearing she'd one day abandon him and explore on her own, he desired a permanent commitment. He wanted the noise of children one day—his and hers.

"Would you ever consider it?" he asked yesterday evening. "Marrying me?"

She'd been slicing tomatoes in the kitchen, and she slapped down her knife. "You have to stop seeing me as a child first," she said. She glared at him for several seconds before resuming slicing with a dangerous vehemence.

Hurt, he left the kitchen for his study. He heard Sara bagging the trash and opening the front door. And then she cried out, calling for Pepper. His border collie had escaped.

They hunted for nearly an hour before they found Pepper huddled in a ditch, her face triple its normal size and hives covering her head, chest, and legs. She'd either been stung by an insect or pricked by a cactus. He rushed his dog home, hoping her throat wouldn't swell before he could administer the allergy shot.

"Do you know what can happen to a dog out in the desert?" he yelled, louder than he meant to. "I told you to watch that she never runs out."

Sara cringed. "You overprotect her."

It led to their fiercest fight: the apex of those that occurred before it. Sara accused him of babying her, not treating her as an equal, being controlling. He stormed off to the back porch. Through the window he heard her crying. When he entered the bedroom two hours later, her suitcase sat on the bed, zipped and packed.

He backed down, apologized, made promises—anything to stop her from leaving. They stayed awake late, Pepper sprawled in a drugged sleep at their feet. Desperate to make amends, he begged her to go climbing the next morning. "I'll take you to one your favorites," he said. "And you can lead it." A pledge he immediately wished to retract.

"As long as it's over a 5.11," she said, her chin thrust forward, victorious.

The trail before them narrowed. Streaks of vermillion materialized behind remote hills. They passed clusters of gnarled gnomes—the Joshua trees Sara praised as beautiful during the brightness of day. In the low light, he knew, they made her nervous.

"Can't you almost imagine them coming to life, drawing us too deep into the desert?" she said of the twisted, spiny silhouettes.

Ashoke paused briefly, puzzled. His mind didn't work that way. He peered at the trees, wanting to understand.

Then his attention shifted to what lay ahead: plutonic mounds of granite gathered into a mountain, looming as if some prehistoric beast. Boulders atop boulders, hundreds of feet high, rounded and sculpted. He'd climbed many of them. The geodesic domes seemed to lean away, as if withholding their joints and cracks, their coarseness, their treacherous façades, from his probes and penetrations.

Ashoke spotted three climbers bustling amidst the indigo shadows of the mountain's western base, their forms miniaturized by the immensity of the rocks. When he drew closer, he noticed the men had already racked their gear and set up top ropes along the curved cliff side, occupying the tough routes Sara planned to lead-climb. He cursed under his breath.

"We should've gotten here sooner."

"Seriously? Earlier than this?" Sara said, the defensive tone of her voice unmistakable.

They stopped less than a hundred feet from where the men worked in the near dark. Two of them, heavily laden with clinking metal equipment, moved out of sight. The third man sat on a folding chair, a wisp of smoke rising through the air above him. Even in silhouette, Ashoke recognized him: Brett, an independent climbing instructor. He hadn't seen Brett for over two years—not since the man had married a Thai client and gone to live with her in Thailand. Several weeks ago, he'd heard one of the guys at the shop mention it. Brett had gotten a divorce and moved back. A nasty affair, from the sound of it.

Ashoke and Brett had a disagreement the last time they interacted, a few months before he met Sara. Ashoke had brought two beginners to one of the park's rare easy top roping spots. When he arrived, Brett had already set up eight ropes spanning the wall's length for his group of students. Ashoke asked Brett to remove a few to make room for his clients' ropes. Brett refused. They argued, and in the end Ashoke had to find a less suitable place.

Now, it was happening again. Until Brett removed his ropes, they couldn't do the routes for which they'd prepared.

He walked to Brett's chair, towering over him. "I heard you were back in town."

Brett tipped back his hat. He had the weathered skin and the starburst of wrinkles around his eyes like most experienced climbers. "Ashoke. It's been a while." He didn't stand or smile.

"What time did you get here?"

"We camped nearby. It's what you gotta do to get what you want."

"I know how to get what I want," Ashoke said, "without hogging all the climbs." He felt Sara behind him, her hand against his lower back urging him to relax.

He looked at Brett's lean and hardened body, his scabbed and corded arms. Despite being over forty, Brett's hair, though peppered with gray, sprang thickly from a hairline not yet receding. His low sideburns accentuated a prominent and still-youthful jaw. Exactly the kind of older man, Ashoke imagined, Sara might find attractive.

Ashoke ran a hand through his own abundant hair, dark enough to mask the gray. He needed Sara with him, here, at this location. He needed her to remember ten months ago, at twilight. He'd finished her lessons, and they were cleaning up. A coyote, its famished body low to the ground, streaked out from behind a yucca. Its tail brushed Sara's leg. Startled, Sara leapt up and collided with Ashoke's chest. Before he could process what was happening, they were stretched on a slab of rough stone, laughing, her hands in his hair, her mouth pressed to his. White flowers glowed on the arms of nearby saguaros, reflecting the moon's luminescence—as did Sara's lunar-pale neck, her shoulders, her breasts. The blooms' scent wafted over them as he supped from her mouth, drinking her in as if from a well. Her limbs opened like petals. It was their first sexual experience together. The moon had traveled halfway across the sky before they'd swayed back to his truck, fingers entwined.

How could she remember that night with Brett in the way? How could they reenact it?

Brett turned back to preparing his rack. Sara stepped closer. Ashoke hated how Brett raked his gaze up and down her body.

"You going to be on those routes for long?" she asked.

"Much of the day," Brett said, leaning back to better study Sara, the elongated grooves at the sides of his mouth deepening. "We usually climb on the south side, near my new place. This time, my clients wanted to try up here for a change. They've done the routes on the other side, and need something advanced."

"So do we," Ashoke said. The muscles tensed at the base of his jaw, making his head hurt.

Sara grabbed his arm. He resisted, then let her pull him forty feet away. They couldn't get much farther because at this part of the mountain, the cliff face bowed inward, leaving an intimate semi-circle of ground from which the climbs started. He didn't want to get into it with Brett in front of her.

The muffled shouts of the two other men, distorted by distance and rocks, blew to them on a breeze. Then, from afar: an animal's plaintive wail, its howl dwindling to a whimper.

"Let's leave," Sara said.

Ashoke scanned the concave wall. "What about the one over there?" He put a hand on Sara's shoulder and indicated an unclaimed route: off-width, riddled with fractures, cluttered with bushes sprouting from cracks. "It's a 5.6."

"What's the point?" She brushed his hand away. "That kiddie route? It's not going to prepare me for anything. And I can't even lead it—there aren't any good spots to place protection."

Brett, bent forward on his folding chair, didn't seem shy about listening with more than casual interest. Ashoke followed the arc of Brett's cigarette from hand to mouth.

Sara said, "It's still early. How about we head to Tahquitz instead—do something different for a change?"

"We can't go there now," Ashoke said, his words echoing. Tahquitz Mountain, known for run-out slabs, multi-pitch crags, and stretchy traverses, often required long approaches. And it was too far a drive. Sara was being willfully impractical, making no sense. "Plus, I'd need at least five or six more cams and more stoppers—a full trad rack, really, to do anything worthwhile."

Sara said nothing. A stubborn curve shaped her lower lip. Her pouts drove him crazy. He sighed. "Look, Sara. Relax. We'll do it next time. Let's just set up here—top rope some routes and then go get dinner. Relish Deli? Or maybe Pie In The Sky for pizza?"

He didn't wait for her to object. He moved closer to the cluster of rocks lining the bottom of the cliff, his footsteps disturbing the sand, leaving marks. Dropping his gear bag, he rummaged through it for webbing, slings, cordelettes. Sara stood with her bag in her arms. She rolled her eyes, then came near him and lowered it as well. He stroked his fingers through her hair; goosebumps rose on her neck.

He said, "I'll go build the anchor."

"Want me to stay here or come with you?"

Ashoke considered this. Meticulous at anchor setting—bombproof, three point, redundant, equalized, perfect-by-the book each time—he refused to use bolts, webbing, or rope left by previous climbers. Instead, he searched for large boulders, thick tree trunks, or other immovable objects upon which to secure his anchor. He preferred to concentrate while constructing it in peace, which he knew might take a while. Brett hadn't budged from his chair and continued to observe them.

"No need for you to hang out here by yourself," Ashoke said. "Unless you'd rather."

"I'll help you. Maybe I can do it this time?"

He didn't say no. But he wasn't planning to let her.

Brett tapped a pack of cigarettes against his palm. When Ashoke and Sara were almost ready, he flipped open his lighter, its click audible in the clean morning. "Climb's you're doing's no good," he said. "Low quality. Bad ascent and descent. Hey, have fun, though. I'll catch you guys later."

"Thanks," Ashoke said. He lowered his voice, but not much. "But we didn't ask you."

Sara shoved him, lightly.

They scouted on the north side of the mountain, which the sun had not yet infiltrated. Ashoke strained to see a possible route up. Sara pointed to a massive diagonal slab comprising one side of a darkly shaded, gaping crevice. A crack ran along the inclined slab, its configuration forming a sketchy path possibly usable by an experienced climber. Without asking Ashoke for his opinion, she hopped onto it. Pressing her fingers and smearing her small shoes against its surface, she scrambled along the crack, moving fast. She hesitated on an outcropping creating a narrow ledge about fifty feet up from where they'd started. The crack leading to the top branched to its right. Above the ledge, a twenty-foot face provided a potential shortcut to avoid a section of the less steep path.

"Fifth class face," Ashoke said when he saw her contemplating it. "You can't do it unroped."

"You could run up this asleep," she argued. "It's barely slanted and has bomber holds. And it'll save us time."

"Barely by whose definition?" he said as he paused below her. "Careful. It's too exposed."

She never listened to him. He wanted to yell at her, to insist she come down immediately. If he did, she'd resent him. He too often questioned her decisions, despite them being usually sound. He knew it upset her. But she'd stayed awake late because of Pepper and their resulting argument. She might not be in the right state to make decisions.

He edged along the crack, thinking he'd meet her where their ascents intersected.

She'd almost finished scaling the small face when a knob she weighted broke loose in her hand. Fighting to maintain her footing, she hooked her toe onto a lip of rock. It crumbled and came unattached.

Losing her balance, she struggled to self-arrest, digging in her fingers and toes to break her descent. She kept sliding. He sprang toward her as she stifled a scream. He was too far to her right.

He heard a grunt. Brett was poised on the ledge, clutching Sara's shirt. He'd caught her before she slipped past the ledge and tumbled down the incline.

"I got her," Brett said. "She's okay." He started backing down the slab with one hand supporting Sara. Though their synchronized movements were cautious and measured, Ashoke guessed there was something wrong with Sara's right foot. He downclimbed quickly.

Sara's face was wet when he joined them at the bottom.

"I'm sorry," she said, a crumpled doll in Brett's hands. She squirmed; it didn't affect his grip. She winced and touched the bruised purple skin near her ankle.

Ashoke smelled campfire in Brett's clothes. Sara probably liked it—she loved camping. He forced his arm between Brett and Sara, circled her waist, and drew her away as gently as possible. She stumbled and swore. He soon had her. "How'd you end up below her?" he asked.

"I was behind you," Brett said. "I thought the route you chose wasn't the best way to the top. I felt better making sure you made it."

It wasn't me who chose the route, Ashoke thought but didn't say.

Sara pushed Ashoke's restraining arm away and tried hopping forward on one foot. Ashoke scooped her off her feet and carried her back to their bags, her feet dangling off his arm.

"I feel like a goddamn toddler," she said.

He refused to release her—she'd pretend it didn't hurt and twist it worse.

Brett reopened his folding chair and brought it to where they'd left their gear. Ashoke lowered her into it. Brett leaned back and lit a joint. He and Ashoke stood facing her, their backs against the uneven wall.

"Mind if I have a drag?" Sara asked. Brett lifted the joint to her and she took it.

She never smoked marijuana with Ashoke.

Sara raised the fresh joint and inhaled, peace coming over her face. After taking a couple more hits, she groped for Ashoke's hand and pressed it to her heart. He kept it there, feeling the warmth of her breath, the rise of her young breasts, the steady movement of her chest. He didn't want to remove it—not now or ever. He knew he'd never climb again, never set foot in a desert, and never manage to find a way to live if she'd bypassed the ledge and slid fifty feet along the slab to the bottom of the crevice.

Brett cleared his throat. Sara shook Ashoke off.

"Thank you," she said, returning the joint to Brett. He flashed his teeth in a grin.

They matched, Ashoke thought, a pain shooting through him. Their skin gleamed white in the early morning, while his brownness absorbed the dark. Ashoke scowled at the joint's damp end. He didn't want the man's lips touching where hers had been.

"You can have more," Brett said. He pinched it, glowing, between finger and thumb.

"No, I mean thank you for back there," Sara said. "What I did—I was being stupid."

Her expression resembled devotion—the emotion he wanted for himself. He knew he should be grateful to Brett. Yet, he couldn't suppress his frustration with himself for not preventing what had happened. It was more than frustration:

what he felt was anger.

"You going to be okay with that ankle?" Brett asked.

"She'll be fine," Ashoke said.

"It's better already." The edges of Sara's lips tilted up at Brett, who basked in the brilliance of that smile. "My name's Sara, by the way," she said. "I get the sense Ashoke knows you? I'm not sure why he didn't introduce me." She looked pointedly at Ashoke.

Brett told her his name, said he was pleased to meet her. *I bet he is*, Ashoke thought.

"She'll be fine," he repeated to Brett.

Sara's gaze fixed on the sky, now cerulean blue splashed with purple and yellow, shifting, incandescent.

"It's Venus," she said, though Ashoke wasn't sure to whom. "So close."

"She's happy now," said Brett. The smoldering joint in his hand had shrunken to a stub.

Venus blinked in the vastness above Sara. "She's had enough," Ashoke said. "I'll take it from here."

"It's helping her, you know. It'll lighten the pain. Let her unwind, get over the fear."

Ashoke said, "I can help her more."

"You've got a nice girl there," Brett said softly, leaning into Ashoke. "But I'm sure you know that."

"Yes," Ashoke made his voice sharp enough to cut. "You can be sure I do." His shoulders hunched toward his ears and the muscle tick in his jaw twitched erratically.

Brett winked at Sara. "You all have a good day," he said more loudly. "I've got to see what those two students of mine are up to. I told them to check out my anchor placement, and they've gone and disappeared on me."

His heels kicked up dust as he walked away, the tiny red speck smoldering in his fingers visible through the dim lavender light.

Ashoke sat on a sloping rock near Sara's feet, his legs spread wide to keep him steady. For a long while he didn't move or speak. Then, as if breaking a trance, he ran the back of his fingers gently along Sara's leg.

"Pepper must be waking up about now," Sara said out of

nowhere. "She'll be wanting her walk."

"I can carry you back to the car," he said. "We can go home."

"I want to climb."

He gave a short laugh. "You're kidding. How're you supposed to climb one-legged? And you're high."

Around them, slow sunlight painted peaks orange. It seemed as if the tops of boulders were aflame. Sara didn't speak again until the blaze had spread lower on the soaring rock formations, awakening the landscape bit by bit, transforming it into burnished copper.

"I only had a few drags," she said. "You can't keep me from going up."

"I don't keep you from doing anything," he said. "Or, if I do, I don't mean to."

"No," Sara said. "I don't think you mean to." She shifted her weight and grimaced.

"We need to leave."

"Ashoke," Sara said.

When she said his name her voice resounded with brutal clarity in the brisk desert air. His stomach lurched and he nearly wept. He wanted to hear her say his name for the rest of his life.

"Can you get me some of those power bars we brought?" she said, her tone now deliberately light. "I'm ready for breakfast."

"Breakfast I'm okay with," Ashoke said. "You climbing—not okay."

"I know." Sara leaned over and wrapped a strand of his hair around her finger, releasing it slowly.

They ate in silence. Her eyes remained fixed on the cliff, eyebrows drawn, as if she were trying to plot her ascent despite being unable to see the holds. Ashoke gathered the wrappers and carefully put them in a bag, which he tied and placed into his pack. He stood and brushed the crumbs off his pants, then offered his hand to help Sara.

She said, "I need to replace the image." Instead of rising, she placed her hand in his, his palm and fingers dwarfing hers. "Sliding down the slab. That can't be what I take from this day."

Ashoke knelt and lightly touched her hurt ankle. She flinched. "Swollen," he said.

A lizard, frantic, zigzagged past a stunted Joshua tree.

Ashoke strode over to his backpack and extracted a roll of ace wrap. Propping the backpack to give her foot a place to rest, he circled her leg twice with the wrap to anchor it, and then expertly created repeating infinity loops around her ankle and calf. He could feel her relax as the wrap provided some comfort. Pushing on her toe, he waited for the white spot to become pink to make sure it was tight, but not too tight, around the foot, and then checked to ensure the wrap loosened as it climbed her calf. Though the sky had lightened, they remained shaded by the cliff.

When he was done, he traced the scratches the fall had left on her arms and legs. She bent forward and grasped his face with her hands. "You need to let me do this." Her pupils were dilated; her lashes, dark at the roots, faded to blonde at the tips. "It's only top roping. It's not like I'm lead-climbing and risking a big fall. You'll have me covered the whole time."

His hands shook when he put away the wrap. "I'm sorry I let you down," he said, turning away. "I should've been spotting you." If he'd kept his hands under her as she free-climbed the shortcut, she might not have fallen.

"I went too high for you to spot me. I let myself down," she said. "The pain will remind me so I won't do it again." She released him and rose, weighting only her uninjured foot. "Can you help me closer to the start?"

She leaned heavily on him as they moved toward the ropes the other men had set up. Brett was nowhere to be seen. He'd likely followed his students around the back of the cliff, toward their anchors. Ashoke surveyed Brett's limp, dangling ropes.

"This one's the most accessible," Sara said, touching one of them. "I'm sure he won't care."

"We're not using his. You insist on climbing, we'll get your rope ready."

She nodded. Ashoke brought her the chair and the bound loops of the new rope. He knelt with it curled around him and gave her one end. It was stiff; they massaged it with their hands to knead out the kinks. She breathed through her mouth, slightly raspy, the way she did when aroused. He felt the energy radiating between them as her slender fingers unraveled the coils of blue. They worked together without speaking.

When the rope was primed and ready, he said, "You'll have to remain here while I set up an anchor."

"I'll wait," Sara said.

A half hour later, he hurtled the rope down the mountain; it unfurled to exactly the right length. Another fifteen minutes and he was back at her side. The rope he'd lowered appeared, in the fuchsia and rose sunrise, as a thin line of sky shooting through the center of the cliff, splitting it open.

"You sure about this?"

"The biggest danger? I bump my foot," she said. "Not a huge deal. This climb isn't hard."

She rested against the wall, raising her hurt foot. Beneath her, globemallow flowers dotted the edges of stones like drops of blood. He tied a figure eight near the end of the rope he'd dropped, ran the section below the knot through the front loop of her harness, and then doubled back over the eight and tied an additional safety knot, imitating the infinity loops he'd done with the ankle wrap. She put on her helmet; he tightened the strap.

He checked the points of her harness for security, and then he put a bite of rope through his belay device and held it in position.

"On belay?" she asked, as he had taught her.

"Belay on," he said. "I'll keep it taut. You won't fall more than a few inches. Tell me when you want to come down."

Sara burrowed her fingers into her chalk bag, coating them completely, and then placed her hands on the cold wall, searching for solid holds. She'd need to use her arms much more than normal. He wasn't sure she had the strength.

"Climbing," she said.

"Climb on," he replied, his voice hoarse with doubt.

It took three tries for her to pull herself a foot off the ground. She bit her lip hard to block what he knew was a significant pain in her ankle. She positioned her good foot on a thin ledge, bent her knee, and then, as she straightened her leg, she stretched up with her hand. Jumping her foot onto a new nub, she leaped again, reaching higher than he thought possible. He hadn't realized the strength she contained within her slight limbs. Her jerky movements took on a rhythm Ashoke found strangely graceful.

Sara's fingers kept returning to the chalk bag to absorb any moisture from her hands that might cause her to slip off. Her single, laboring leg shook from the strain, as did her arms, which must be burning, painful and hot. His own arms burned in sympathy. She was drenched; sweat stained her shirt's underarms and lower back. The section she climbed remained shaded as the horizontal wave of light from the sun flowed steadily downward to meet her.

Ashoke craned his head trying to observe her, feeling the strain in the tendons of his neck and behind his shoulders. He yanked the rope rapidly through his hands, keeping time with Sara's jumps to remove any slack, and shouted the locations of holds she might need, his voice bouncing off the wall. He'd belayed thousands of times before. None felt as exhausting as this. Sweat dripped into his eyes; he blinked it away. He didn't dare let go with his left hand long enough to wipe his face, even with his right hand in locked position when Sara paused, which she did increasingly often.

At last, Sara's head emerged from shadow into the radiant red of the sun. She smiled at him, the shivers of her muscle spasms visible even from where he stood. When she lost her next hold and came off the rock, he was ready and the rope stayed firm. She paused, hanging from her harness, panting from the surprise of the fall. She was trembling. He called to her, asking if she wanted to quit. She didn't respond, but instead reached for the wall and kept climbing.

As she got higher, he stopped yelling suggestions. He wanted to scamper behind her and put his hands beneath her foot to support her and ease her ascent. He wanted to grasp her waist, his fingers pressing into her soft, warm flesh, and lift her step by step. Most of all, he longed to watch her forever as she grew closer to him, even while moving farther away.

Not far from the top, she leaned back, extending her arms wide as though an upside down eagle, her good foot flat against the wall and her body hovering in air. Her gesture showed him what he wanted to know: that she trusted him completely. He held her suspended with all the care he could muster. When she was ready, she reached for the rock again and kept going.

.

This Road May Flood

Kari Shemwell

The day after Thanksgiving we drive out to Land Between the Lakes to search for the drowned man, though we are less interested in finding him than we are eager to escape our house.

In town, we stop for a bag of cheese curds. We sit in the car watching Black Friday shoppers carry armfuls of lotions and DVDs across the strip mall parking lot while we separate the greasy cheese balls onto two napkins. You say, "Some of mine are still frozen in the middle," and I say, "Unlucky." The afternoon shoppers have risen far too late for the laptops and flat-screen televisions, and we admire them, claiming that we, too, would never stay up all night to take part in such ugly consumerism, even if we could afford the glossy sales bill prices. Before driving away, we touch hands, because even though last week you had to sell your grandfather's antique shotgun after I put it under my chin, it's still comforting to feel our fingers together.

The man drowned almost seventy years ago, so the story goes. Before it was a National Recreation Area, Land Between the Lakes was farmland. There were also some villages, and no lakes, until they dammed up the Cumberland River to create the two bodies of water and the land between. The communities were drowned. Almost everyone took buyouts and moved away, but a few crazies stood their ground and drowned along with their homes like captains of sinking ships. If only they had known how little it mattered. Everyone's grandparents eventually lost their farms and moved to Detroit to take up with Ford or GM, anyway.

We skip the new bypass and drive the old highway that bends through naked forests. It's a cold day, the sky wiped blank as a sheet by flat, shapeless clouds. You don't speak. We cross the rusted, two-lane bridge that has just reopened. It was struck by a barge last year. The county keeps promising to build a second bridge—four lanes—to allow more tourists to travel to the Land Between the Lakes. The truth is that there have never been enough tourists to fill the current bridge. We pull off the highway and park on a gravel road blocked by an iron gate. You get out and look up and down the lake's shoreline, checking the bank for wildlife, mostly eagles and wolves that no one ever spots. I get out and tighten my hat to protect against the wind whipping across the choppy water. Your hair is blown flat against your forehead, and though your words are carried away on the wind, I can see your lips shaping the question: Where should we start?

*   *   *

Last month we went to a post-Halloween get together at my professor's house. He and his wife had a new chemical they wanted us to try, and they assured us that, with our masters programs ending soon, it would leave nothing in our hair follicles to be detected during drug screenings. We watched a Tim Burton film because the professor's wife still had black and orange lights strung around the entertainment center and a leftover bowl of candy for trick-or-treaters.

When we could feel our heads floating, the professor and his wife started talking about the drowned man. People had reported seeing him in the woods for decades, but sightings were few and far between, and mostly old tales. But, lately, they said, the drowned man had been sighted more and more often, mostly sitting on the bank of Goat Island.

"You know," the professor said, "There are still roads and

chimneys under the water." He talked with his hands moving, like he always had something to teach you. "Houses, stores, and train tracks at the bottom of the lake."

His wife, a tall, skinny woman with black hair like motor oil, emerged from the bathroom where she had just finished hurling. "Cemeteries, too," she said, then laughed. "This stuff always makes me vomit."

"Why does he hang around?" I asked. "There's nothing out there but wilderness."

"Because it's his home, I guess." The professor drank wine so much that his lips were always purple. "We saw him while driving over Barkley Bridge last weekend."

"You didn't stop?"

"Of course not, it was raining and the gravel had flooded."

"I was afraid," said the professor's wife.

I turned to you to see what you thought about the drowned man, but you were already gone. Your face was pale and you had flown elsewhere. The professor offered you a glass of water and said, "Take deep breaths." I held onto your hand, hoping if I touched your skin I might be able to see what you saw. I worried you might be ill except you were smiling. You always managed to glide into a colorful, artificial landscape when we got high, while I sunk into stew and vanished, sometimes for days. I could feel the separation. You rising, glowing, and me capsizing, flannel coating my mouth and filling my throat. I hoped you would hold on to me, not let me go down, but instead the professor's wife put her skinny, cold hands on my forehead and whispered, "It's all right."

*   *   *

By the time we reach Goat Island, our noses have turned red, but the cold air feels more appropriate outside than within a home, so we don't mind it much. Logs have collected in the shallow water between the bank and the island, making it easy to walk from the mainland without getting wet. In the summer we would know to stay far away from a patch of snake-infested branches in the lake, but in the winter we feel safe enough.

I say, "Don't go too fast." The bottoms of my shoes are worn flat and slippery, so I'm not as sure-footed on the logs. I ask to hold your arm.

"No," you tell me, "it would only make us both fall."

I know you are right. I remember the time you asked me why I was so afraid to stay alone overnight at our home. I said it was because we lived so far out in the woods, making us a target for criminals. Burglars and murderers know police can't respond quickly to homes out in the country. You told me it wouldn't be any better if you were there with me, that you couldn't protect us from bullets or knives. I asked, "But don't you think the idea of dying with someone you love is more comforting than the idea of dying alone?"

You shook your head and said, "Why would you want the person you love to die, too, when it could just be one of you?"

On the island we have to climb and push through tangled brush. The thorns catch my sleeves and pant legs. I can feel the cuts and tiny smears of blood beneath the fabric of my thin jeans. Burs and twigs stick to your jacket, in your hair. I reach toward you to pick the pieces off. When you feel my fingers, you stop to let me remove the debris. I pull you around to face me. For a moment, we look into each other's eyes. I can see that you are searching for emotion, just like me, but the moment is too forced. We can feel the fabrication.

We reach the far side of the island. Upon emerging from the brambles, we look toward the lake and see an old man standing with his feet in the water.

You say, "I think that's him."

I search the pebbled bank for his shoes, but see none.

You say, "You think he's getting his shoes wet?"

And I smile because we are still in some ways alike.

We stand watching him for a moment. His long gray beard waves like a ribbon in the wind. He isn't exactly frightening, but something about his pose stalls us—chin down, arms barely lifted from his sides, palms upturned, so still he could be a corpse propped up.

I say, "He's not totally of this world."

You say, "That sounds like the Syfy channel."

And I say, "Or church."

You always think that you are the brave one, the one who doesn't mind sleeping alone, the one who will stand too close to the edge of a bluff or drive without power-steering in our old busted Cadillac, but I am the one who approaches the drowned man. You stand behind me with your hand on my back. When we get close enough to see his bluish-gray skin and the algae on his clothes, you grab my hand.

*   *   *

When we were ready to leave the professor's house, we still couldn't operate a vehicle. I said, "Please, let's go see the Christmas lights at the park."

You said, "You're supposed to drive through them."

I tugged your sleeve. "We can walk."

The professor's wife ran to the kitchen, singing "you'll-need-canned-goods-to-enter" to the tune of The Christmas Song, but the rhythm was a little off and she abandoned it after the first line. She brought back four jars of pickled okra and said, "My mother makes these and we hate them."

At the park, after depositing our jars in the drop box, you said, "Why do they start this so early? We still have our pumpkins out."

"More canned goods, I guess." I took your hand in mine as we walked past a two-dimensional Santa sled, but you wouldn't return my grip. The legs of the reindeer moved back and forth. Rudolph wore a blue Wildcats hat.

"Dead fish," I said.

You looked at me funny.

"That's what you always whisper to me when you shake someone's hand and they don't grip. Dead Fish."

"Oh, yeah. I hate that."

I pointed at our conjoined hands with my free one.

You looked, too, then began to squeeze my hand until I had to pull away.

"Stop," I said. "That hurts."

"Isn't that what you want?" You shrugged and stepped off the pavement to stand next to wise men under a giant star. The speakers played the version of "Rudolph The Red-Nosed

Reindeer" that always reminded us of the California Raisins.

"What's that supposed to mean?"

You shook your head. "I don't know."

"You're high," I said.

"So what? You're low. You're always low."

I stood on the opposite side of the pavement. "I know."

Red and green lights alternated across your face, like they were saying "stop, go, stop, go," but really just trying to say "Merry Christmas."

You said, "I don't know what to do anymore. It's like I can't even touch you."

"I know."

We started walking again.

You said, "If you're not all right, you should stop doing drugs."

"You're probably right."

We walked past a cutout of the Grinch struggling under the weight of a giant bag of presents.

"Your chemicals are already fucked up enough."

I said, "Tell me about it."

*   *   *

We both look at the drowned man in reverent silence, as though he is a priest behind a sliding door. He is very old and leeches suck his elbows. His clothes are cotton and most assuredly hand-stitched to have lasted so long under the muddy water. Up close, he is not so scary, not even as tall as you. His feet have been pulled deep into the mud. We stare at him long enough to feel comfortable.

Finally, I say, "Hello, sir. Have you drowned?" just to be sure that it's really him, and you look at me as if I've said something rude. I shrug.

The drowned man turns his head slightly toward us, and says, "A long time ago."

"Is there anything we can do to help you?" I ask.

He says, "How can you get anything done with your hands all tied up like that?"

You look at your wrist, then mine, and confirm that they

are indeed unbound. I shrug again.

The drowned man begins to laugh and I laugh, too, because now I am afraid of being rude.

You say, "We could drive you somewhere, sir. Anywhere you want to go. We have towels in the car."

The drowned man sits down in the sand and ignores you. I sit down next to him and look out over the water, trying to see what he sees. The wet mud seeps into the seat of my pants.

"Where's your family?" I say. "You do have a family, don't you?"

The drowned man coughs and brown water runs down his chin. He rubs his hands together as though he is warming them over a fire. He says, "I had a wife and two daughters. They were sweet as honeysuckle."

I can taste the wet centers of the blossoms on my tongue. The drowned man watches a hawk dive toward a patch of grass on the opposite bank. I put my hand on his shoulder and pat, as if to say, there, there. You look at me weird, like I've touched a bloated corpse.

I say, "What happened?"

The drowned man scoops pebbles into his hands. "They've gone on some place else now," he says. "I had to stay behind. If you're going to drown for something, you've got to stay."

You lean down and whisper into my ear, "He's not making any sense."

I don't really understand the drowned man, either, but I want to sit with him for a while and try to make sense of it all. "He's all alone," I say to you.

The drowned man turns to me and smiles. His teeth are yellowed with brown spots on them. There is lake scum drying in his eyebrows and mustache. He reaches toward me. I can sense you going stiff, ready to pounce if something bad happens. But, the drowned man only puts his palm on my cheek. His skin is cold and damp, so waterlogged that it feels like a catfish on my face. He has the smell of lake water, both dead and alive, dirty and clean at the same time.

*   *   *

Last week, we rode into the city with the professor and his wife to go to a couple's club. This was the sort of place with no sign and a password. You were expected to pay $100 each for admission and consider switching partners once inside.

The professor's wife had said, "We aren't interested in that part, really. We are just curious."

"We aren't interested in that, either," I said. "We'll think about it."

We had decided to go, agreeing that the professor and his wife must have hit a rough patch, and what are friends for, right?

At home, you said, "I've heard it's like a maze inside and people go nude."

I said, "It's never the ones you want to see nude."

And you said, "Well, now we have to go."

At the club, the professor and his wife danced to an electronic song while a strobe light turned their motions robotic. She wore something silky like a nightie and he had gotten down to baggy boxers and a white tank top that he had sweated through. They took tablets when we arrived, and when they offered us some, you said, "No, thank you," and pinched my side.

I said, "Not tonight," and sat at the bar.

We sipped drinks until the professor and his wife disappeared down a hallway with a group of people wearing Mardi Gras masks.

You said, "We hate clubs."

And I said, "Yeah, we do."

You took my hand and led me through a crowd of people jerking and shaking to an eighties song. Down another hallway, we found a small, dark room with three rows of velvet seats and brown curtains on the walls. No one was inside, so we sat down together in the middle row facing a projection screen. The screen lit up and began playing a pornography reel.

You said, "This is what porn looks like when you actually pay for it."

I said, "I bet people have had sex on these seats."

"Gross."

We sat in silence while the screen showed a woman confronting her husband's mistress, only to end up being seduced by her as well.

I tried to make a joke. "Everyone loves girl-on-girl," I said, but you weren't listening to me. You weren't even looking at the screen. You were thinking of something else altogether.

You said, "Promise me you won't do anything stupid," but it sounded like a question. You looked like a wounded animal in your seat, like you could see me lying cold in the bathtub already.

I wanted to kiss your neck and say, "No, of course not," but I didn't want to lie to you. So I said, "How could I know it was stupid?"

You wouldn't look at me. The screen lit up your face.

"People don't know things are stupid before they do them. Why would they do them if they did?"

You never answered, but on Monday, when you got home from work, I saw you sit in the car for fifteen minutes before coming inside, just staring at the windshield like you wished you could fall asleep.

*   *   *

On the bank, the wind begins to pick up and the flat sky separates into clumps of black clouds.

"Yesterday was Thanksgiving," you say from behind us.

The drowned man says, "I don't remember that day."

You say, "Oh."

I remember the professor and his wife and the things they said about the worlds beneath the lakes.

I say, "Is it true that there are roads and train tracks under the water? Our friends want to know."

The drowned man holds my hand like a prom date. "I can show you if you stay a while."

"No," you say. "There's no place on earth more dangerous to dive than these lakes. The water is so muddy that you can't see your hand in front of you. People sometimes get clobbered by logs out of nowhere."

"Really?" I ask.

"Really," says the drowned man. "I've buried some of their bodies myself. In the cemeteries on the bottom of the lake."

You kick at the grainy sand. You ask, "Why would you do such an awful thing?" You sound angry. "Then they'll never be found. What about their families?"

The drowned man drops his head and shakes it back and forth. "No one's family should see that."

You say, "This guy's crazy. Let's go."

But I'm not ready to leave yet. The drowned man has put his other hand around my wrist and plays with the sleeve of my jacket. He slides his finger under the cuff then out again, softly, the way you touch the ones you love.

I say to you, "Go on. You can come back for me tomorrow."

You begin walking back and forth. You stop to pick up a rock then throw it into the water. It makes a desperate gulping sound when it sinks. You say, "Are you crazy, too? You can't stay here all night. It's going to rain. You'll freeze."

You're right. We can all see the storm churning on the horizon.

You begin to shake my shoulders, saying, "He's probably going to kidnap you or worse. You can't stay here."

I know you are right, but the drowned man is still holding my hand. His palms are so wet I can feel my skin pruning up under his grip. I'm afraid that he might not let go, but I'm also scared that he will.

"Just a little longer," I say. "You can wait in the car."

"Jesus fucking Christ," you say, but you sound hurt instead of mad. "I'm not leaving you here with this lunatic."

And you wait.

I can hear your feet crunching the rocky bank behind us as you shift your weight back and forth. Eventually the wind howls so loudly that it swallows your noise. For a moment, I think you have left, until I feel your breath on my neck and your arms slide around my waist. You stay that way until the drowned man releases my hand. He stands and walks into the water. When he has walked so far that his chin skirts the surface, he says, "There are cities under here, believe it," then disappears beneath the waves.

*   *   *

One night back in the summer, we were driving the old road to our home in the woods during a nasty rainstorm. It had been falling like artillery fire since morning, and we both said, "We should have replaced the wipers when we had the chance."

On Stateline Road, we came upon the dip at the creek where a drainage pipe runs beneath the pavement. The water had risen, spilled over the road and drowned the shrubs and small trees along the stream. We could see the current flowing south, strengthened by the sky dumping buckets down the surrounding hills.

You parked beside a yellow sign on the shoulder.

I read the warning on the sign, and said, "That sounds like poetry."

You got out with your jacket wrapped around your head and walked to the edge of the overflown stream. When you returned, you said, "It's not too deep. We can drive across."

"No," I said. "They say never to cross a flooded part of the road. The current can be way stronger than it looks."

You said, "Who says that?"

"Everyone."

"I just looked. It's fine. This Cadillac weighs a ton."

I was afraid of drowning then. I said, "Please, don't. Once I saw a man's car get swept away on the news."

"You've got to be kidding," you said. "This isn't the Nile." You laughed and put the car in drive. We began to inch across.

I rolled down my window and stuck my head out. The water rose around the tires making a dangerous rushing sound. "Stop," I yelled. "Go back."

You pulled on my hood. "What are you doing? You're soaking the seats." You kept pulling me and telling me to come back inside.

The rain had soaked my hair. You yelled to me as we drove across, but I left the window open so we could swim out if we went under.